# I am J
# I am Paul

## A Story of Two Soldiers in Ancient Rome

### By Mark Tedesco

"For indeed, true friendship is this: it is when two bodies share but one soul."

Aristotle
*Nichomachean Ethics*

To John and Tony

# I am John
# I am Paul

## A Story of Two Soldiers
## in Ancient Rome

By Mark Tedesco

# Table of Contents

There is a basilica on the Cælian Hill in Rome which honors the memory of two men, John and Paul, who fought as soldiers under Emperor Constantine. Underneath is their home, now excavated. The stones still speak of their bond to each other and to their belief.

# Chapter 1: The Dark Road

It is so dim, even with the one lamp that burns, that I can scarcely see my own writing or even my hands. I sit here in a small cell, in what part of Rome I do not know. There are sounds far away: people talking and laughing, muffled by the distance. I long to be among them. But here I am, a prisoner awaiting judgment. What events have come together to lead me here? What will come to pass? Where is Paul? What is happening to him?

My name is Ioannes Fulvius Marcus Romanus; Romanus, because I have lived in Rome since I retired from military duty over twenty years ago.[1] I have devoted my life to the welfare of those in the Empire, and now I am the enemy. I write this not with bitterness, but with disbelief.

As a young boy, I dreamed of joining the legion even as my father dreamed of my being a farmer. While he plowed in the fields, I made swords out of sticks. While he harvested, I was busy weaving the wheat into a shield. "John!" he would call when he needed my assistance. I would run to him, fully armed with wooden sword and straw shield, and challenge him in battle. He would pick me up and swing me around, disarming me, laughing as he did so. "Now how about a hand out here?"

---

[1] Since the names *John* and *Paul* are not of Roman origin, it can be assumed that both men added to their names during their sojourn in Rome.

he would ask.

We lived in a humble home on a small piece of land, enough to sustain my parents, my sister Fulvia, and me. I lost two brothers while they were very young. When my father died it seemed certain that I would never see the legion until Fulvia announced that she had no intention of remaining in the countryside. She convinced our mother to move with her to Rome. Our mother had no objections because she was also ready for a new beginning. I supported this idea. I would then be freed from the obligation to remain on the farm. I could fulfill my dream of becoming a soldier. It was a childlike fantasy I had, as if by defending the greatness of the Empire, my life too could become something important.

Some time after her move to Rome, my sister married and settled into the type of family life that she desired. Because her husband was a man of means, she was able to provide for our mother also, and this set my mind at ease. I was then able to focus my attention more completely on my life within my cohort.

This was the time in which the Empire was ruled by three: Constantine in the north, Maxentius in the south, and Licinius in the east. Although the Empire was one, there had been various leaders since Diocletian established the Tetrarchy.[2] This had become a necessity due to the threats coming from the Germans in the north and the Persians in the east. Without a supreme commander in each area, the Empire was always at a disadvantage in anticipating or responding to enemy aggression. Within our section of the empire our ultimate commander was Constantine. However, neither I nor any soldiers in my century had ever seen him.

Perhaps the road that has led me here started when I met

---

[2] Due to the size of the Empire, Diocletian divided the territory into four sections in 293 C.E., and appointed three others to rule with him. This ruling Tetrarchy consisted of two Caesars and two Augusti, lasting until 313 C.E.

Paulus, or Paul. We were stationed in the same century[3] in Germania. Our camp was in a forested area, with hills to the north, which sometimes put us at a disadvantage. However, the presence of Roman soldiers in this area became necessary. Because the Empire's borders were vulnerable to attack, the task of our division was to secure Roman territory from invasions. This had been a problem since the beginning of the Empire. Even the first Caesar fought many battles against these people. The natives in Germania gather in tribes, which then form armies which seek land and wealth that is not their own.

The inhabitants in those northern areas are coarse, uneducated, and lack Roman virtue as well as military strategy. Although they can be good fighters as individuals, they never form a powerful unit. During one of our patrols, my companions and I were overcome by the invaders who had been hiding in the forest area. We were greatly outnumbered. Men from our century quickly assembled and we were able to drive the enemy back. In battle after battle, I have seen the same Roman military superiority overcome a greater enemy; I believe it is because we fight as one, whereas the others fight together, yet alone.

The effectiveness of our century was hindered by our Commander, Terentianus. He had been appointed leader three years earlier. He was an ill-humored man of medium height, too overweight for the battlefield, with delicate hands, small dark eyes, and a face as round as a barbarian shield. He had obtained the position as centurion through a series of favors, due to his family connections, but he was ill-suited. He probably realized this, for his dream was to have political power in Rome or one of the provinces, and he was often heard complaining about where our century was then stationed. His *Optio*, or second in command,

---

[3] The Roman *centuria*, or century, numbered between eighty and one hundred men. In the Imperial period six centuries made up a cohort and ten cohorts a legion. There is evidence that, by the fourth century, legions operated in detachments of one or two cohorts and some of these became legions in their own right, averaging around one thousand men.

fulfilled the tasks that Terentianus should have seen to.

Our legion was scattered for many miles in an attempt to solidify the borders, so Terentianus was the only commanding officer we ever saw. He could be cruel and heartless. For example, when some *tirones*, or new recruits, arrived he sent three of them in search of a new water source for the soldiers. He purposely sent them in the wrong direction, ordering them not to return until they had completed their mission. When these young and inexperienced men returned to camp seven days later, parched and fearful for their lives, the Commander laughed. This was his sense of humor; this is how he treated his men.

Terentianus, however, was not alone. It is said that the quality of a man can be judged by the friends with whom he surrounds himself. Our Commander was similar to those around him: they were all willing to do anything to attain a more powerful position.

Though our men had no love for our Commander, we were loyal to one another and were determined to fight the enemy and to make sure our entire century would return home. Because so little direction was coming from Terentianus, we organized ourselves into our own groups in preparation for battle, to assure that we would be covered on all flanks. Because I had the confidence of many, I found myself as a leader on the battlefield, issuing orders as if I were a commander. This proved effective in battle, for one was needed who would make quick decisions without waiting for orders. However, Terentianus reprimanded me more than once for "usurping" his authority. Time and again, I listened to his words but did not change my ways, for my safety and that of the men depended on these self-devised tactics.

\*\*\*

Occasionally a skirmish would break out in which those who hated the Empire would attempt to drive us south, for they claimed the lands that we occupied as their own. One night, I was awakened by a sound and an unsettled feeling. I had a sense that something was wrong, although I could hear nothing. I quietly roused the others in my quarters. Following procedure, while we quickly readied ourselves for battle, one of our number awoke those of the adjacent tent, and so on, until about 70 men had been quietly awakened. Suddenly there was a sound not far from our camp; I was sure it was the presence of the enemy. Part of our number made a wide circle, keeping concealed all the while. Very slowly and quietly, the circle closed in, until we routed eight from Germania who held weapons and were ready to fight. Apparently their plan was to penetrate our camp and slay as many of us as possible, tent by tent. Somehow they crept by our sentinel unnoticed. Even in the moonlight I could see that they had the appearance of those from Germania: reddish hair, pale skin, and largely built. As our circle closed in on them I could wait no longer. I was eager to punish Rome's enemies, so I leaped forward to engage them. Others followed. I carried two swords with me. With one, I struck at one enemy's legs, and as he deflected my strike with his shield, I swung with all my might at his face. As I ripped open his throat, I was sprayed with his blood. Others jumped in until a raging fight was taking place. We outnumbered the enemy, however, for they had not anticipated our number and ferocity. We slew them all, in fact, and their bodies were lying at our feet. The fighting had lasted a short time, and we stood there for a moment before looking up and smiling at one another. I felt my dripping, red chest. I looked up as I wore the blood of the enemy with honor. We had triumphed and congratulated ourselves as we carried the bodies and hung them upside down on the frontiers of the enemy. These barbarians must have understood our message, for the bodies were gone the next day, and we had no problems with them for several weeks after.

On another occasion, I lost sight of my comrades and found myself surrounded by the enemy on the battlefield. I had only my sword and shield against seven others. Closing in on me, we all heard a shout, and like a mad man, Paul, whom I did not yet know more than by sight, came plunging down the hillside with screams and shouts and sword. The enemy was shocked and startled; this gave me a moment to engage them with the help of Paul. In a short time they fled, more in terror of Paul than for any other reason. As they withdrew we both laughed; from that moment Paul and I became bound together.

Who is this Paul? He also came from a small town far from Rome; his father was not a soldier and was from humble origins, as was mine. He too lived on a farm as a child, but he lost all of his family at a young age and was raised by his uncle. This was a part of his life that he was hesitant to speak about.

Paul loves battle as much as I do, and his enthusiasm for it, as well as everything he engages in, is contagious. In appearance, he is robust and tall, more like a son of Hercules than a typical soldier. Some are intimidated by him, but despite his strong exterior, Paul is much affected by those he cares about. I have seen him weep for them and rejoice with those who have come into some good fortune. He is prone to be passionate about what he believes in and protective of those he cares about. Of all his passions, however, that of being a soldier is the strongest. There have been those who faulted Paul for what they called his excessive love for combat. He does indeed love to fight, but also to observe battle. This is why gladiatorial fights are also his obsession; although they are forbidden in some places, they are still held throughout the provinces, and more than once he was absent from his camp to attend such a spectacle nearby. For Paul, combat is sport, and he enjoys it exceedingly.

Over the next four years, Paul and I served in the same century together, often training or fighting side by side. We learned each other's methods and strategies to anticipate each other's moves, and almost to read each other's thoughts. I am not sure how this bond between us grew; it was almost like a seedling which one fails to notice until it is already a tree. The link between us was such as this.

Friendship is much honored in the legion, and Paul and I

were respected by the other soldiers. What makes a century indestructible is the loyalty among the men, when one is willing to risk himself for the others. Paul knew I would give my life for him without hesitation, and I knew the same of him; time after time this was exemplified in combat. I remember once when half of our century was sent on an expedition to Gaul. Rome's enemies from Germania had descended into that area and had established camps from which they would take advantage of unguarded travelers as well as pillage villages. Our task was to patrol and secure the areas of unrest until a permanent regiment could be established there.

We arrived and set up our base; we would be stationed here for several months before returning to Germania. After two days, our men were given their tasks and our work divided. We had only a general idea of where the adversary might be. My division was sent to go out and find any signs of enemy presence. Eighty of us fanned out, checking ruins, holes, caves, even piles of stones for signs of this foe. My Commander had issued orders that we were to divide the land into sections and each soldier was to cover his territory alone, reporting by signal if he needed assistance. This was a foolish way to accomplish our task, for it put each one at greater risk, but this mattered not to Terentianus. Hours after the patrols began, I found myself alone, walking among rocks, trees, wildlife, seeing no signs of human presence. Spying a cave in the upper hills, I climbed up and went inside expecting nothing. I suddenly found myself surrounded by at least twelve powerful Germanic marauders. My exit was cut off as several of them who had knives and swords moved in. We stood facing one another for what seemed a long time, as each side contemplated the risk of stepping forward. I was backing up as they were moving forward, when one slipped behind me and lashed out at me from behind, deeply cutting my flesh and muscles in my back. I turned and swung my sword with all my might, hitting the shield of the assailant, but I was quick enough to swing again and disabled him by cutting deep into his arm. The others were upon me when there was a shout which made us all freeze. There was a great clamor, as if an entire cohort was at the entrance of the cave. In fear, the men fled through another exit; I stood there stunned as Paul trampled in, creating an uproar all by himself. It was a tactic I had seen him use in battle to instill fear in his opponent before striking; he always said he learned it from the legends of Hannibal who used elephants to surprise his adversary. Paul used noise and intimidation. I would always remind him that Hannibal was an enemy of Rome and he would laugh. In any case, Paul helped me exit the cave, for I was now bleeding profusely. He briefly pursued the enemy, who fled in fear, thinking that there were more than two of us. "Brother, never do this again, never go off on your own like this! I will see to it that no harm comes to you, but you must help me do so! I know that you would do the same for me." I knew then that I had more than a brother in Paul.

It took me many weeks to recuperate from the slash in my back, for it was deep. I did recover, however, with the help of those in my tent, and also Paul who made sure that I did not endanger myself in my condition.

In those months in Gaul we found several of the enemy camps and were able to capture and also execute those who had been engaged in crimes against Rome. We were relieved, however, when our orders came to return to the area of Germania, which was familiar territory, and was the closest thing to what we could call home.

\*\*\*

A soldier's life is not one of constant battle. Mostly, it is one of waiting. We used this time to prepare, practicing our skills and refining our tactics. Because Paul and I shared an interest in battle, we were always trying to apply Roman ingenuity to new situations. Romans, Paul used to say, are known for their ability to use the power first of the mind, then of the sword. We would spend hours practicing our military craft with our weapons, battling each other or our comrades, but never causing wounds. In the evenings we would challenge each other mentally, as one invented a military situation almost impossible to win, and the other came up with an original solution which would give him the advantage. Paul's solutions were always so predictable; His ingenious fear tactic was making lots of noise before routing the enemy. I reached the point at which I could complete his battle plan before he finished explaining it. "Yes, you shout and bang your shield and then?"

Paul once replied, "I would be no match for you John! Instead of being surprised on the field, you would simply laugh, knowing that I would be behind any loud noise coming at you." We all laughed at this. Yet, despite the humor, Paul was greatly respected because his strength and his decisiveness on the battlefield were a great asset.

\*\*\*

Besides our battle preparation, it was common for the men in our area to attend to the worship of Mithras.[4] Honoring this god gave us hope in our endeavors and increased the bond among us. There were many feasts celebrated around the Mithraeum as we commemorated the birth of Mithras from a rock at the beginning of time. As the god came forth, he carried a torch in one hand and a dagger in the other; from the torch he brought light, while from the knife he would bring life. We also sought to imitate the strength of the god in his slaying of the bull from which the world sprang forth. The miracles of Mithras were also remembered, as when he shot an arrow into a stone and a river gushed forth, thereby bringing the oceans and life and fertility to the earth. We were exhorted to purify ourselves with water and deeds to rid ourselves of evil. Because these stories and others were written in the heavens, we were

---

[4] By the second century C.E. the cult of Mithras had spread throughout the Roman Empire.

instructed to seek them out among the stars.[5]

The celebrations occurred every week on the day of the Sun, and on other particular days set aside. The *pater* [6] of the Mithraeum would invite us to partake of a meal, a ritual consisting of bread and wine, followed by a great feast. Though I was never initiated in Germania, I treasured my belonging to the Mithraeum, for it gave to our century unity, brotherhood, and courage.

***

Occasionally *tirones,* or new recruits, would arrive to join our century, and this was the case with the appearance of Crispus and Crispinianus. They had joined the legion in Malta but were sent to the border cohorts in the north. All thought they were brothers, because they had a similar appearance: darker and shorter than most, black hair and eyes, with quick smiles, and ready to laugh. Though they denied they were related, nobody believed them. If one was present, and the other was missing, it was common to ask, "Where is your brother?" At first this seemed to annoy them, but with the passing of time they became accustomed to it.

Crispus and Crispinianus were younger and less experienced than Paul and I. They were assigned to share our quarters, eight of us in the tent. Their arrival added a new lightheartedness to our dwelling. Crispus in particular was one who would joke with Paul, trying to scare him. Once, when all were falling asleep,

---

[5] Many Mithraic beliefs were based on the constellations, and its seven steps corresponded to the seven planets. Mithras, for example, is represented by the constellation Perseus as he slays the bull, Taurus. The blood running from the slain bull is the Milky Way. The Mithraic cult included creation stories, such as the slaying of the bull from whose blood the universe sprung, to purification rites in which the initiate would be anointed with the blood of the bull. Mithras was seen as the source of all life, who would assure his followers of both happiness in the afterlife, as well as the resurrection of the body.

[6] The head of each Mithraeum was called a *pater*, or father.

Paul was startled by a voice outside of our tent. It seemed like a low growl, half human and half animal. When he went outside to see what it was, there was nobody there. This happened several times until Crispinianus started to laugh. We were all awake by then, looking at one another. Glancing around, we were all bewildered by what was occurring. Crispus was still asleep and did not stir. Paul went over to shake him, but found a bundle of clothes piled up on his cot in the form of a man, covered by a blanket. We all began to laugh as Paul rushed out to try to catch Crispus who had been whispering outside of our tent next to Paul's ear. He chased Crispus down the hillside and up again until Paul caught him and threw him over his shoulder. Other men awoke and all were laughing at the spectacle.

There was another time when we rose in the morning to put on our gear and prepared to go about our duties. When Paul reached for his sword, he found a stick. Although Crispus had already left the tent, we all knew he was behind it, and Paul picked him up and threatened to throw him down a cliff unless he produced the sword. Crispus obliged him, and everyone present, including Paul, laughed for a long time.

These two new men brought a new life into our century. Neither had ever been away from their island, so they were in the legion seeking adventure. We were kindred spirits with Crispus and Crispinianus, so we quickly became friends. I made a special effort to help them to adjust to our century and to avoid the presence of our Commander.

\*\*\*

With the arrival of new recruits, it was commonplace for some men to be able to go to their homes to visit their families. I was hoping to be able to travel to Rome to visit my mother and sister, and was expecting to be released during this time. Word got around that Terentianus had no intention of allowing any of the men to leave. This caused anger in our camp. "What possible reason could he have for keeping us here?" Paul raged. We stood in a group outside of our dwelling with several of our comrades, including several *tirones*. I could think of no military reason for such a decision.

Antonius, a fellow soldier, suggested with disgust, "Perhaps it has to do with our payments. I believe he receives more revenue for himself if he keeps us here." We were all silent, angry at the possibility of his ill-advised conduct. This type of talk was not unusual among us, for our Commander was only respected by those to whom he granted particular favors. The attitude of Terentianus had two effects among the men: it dampened our morale, and yet strengthened the loyalty of soldier to soldier. Perhaps it was the very absence of a qualified commander that increased the bond between us and the sense of responsibility for one another which permeated our regiment.

There were times when the murmuring bordered on rebellion. During this time, word came to me that in various *contuberniums*, or tent groups, my name was being circulated as one who should replace Terentianus. I believe I was favored due to my training the new recruits, as well as often taking a commanding role on the field of battle. Though our Commander had reprimanded me for my initiative, the men had followed my lead, for I was acting for their safety and well being. I did not encourage this talk of my name as commander because such discord would weaken our effectiveness, and sour even more my relationship to Terentianus whom I also tried to avoid at all costs.

\*\*\*

Sergius Sextus had been a friend when I had first entered the legion, and he now held a position of some importance in the military command. His unit arrived one day and remained with our century for one week. It was known that he was on his way to the Emperor at *Augusta Treverorum,*[7] and all were on their best behavior, especially Terentianus. After some days, Sergius and I were able to speak, and he revealed his mission to me. "Terentianus is being considered for an important command, and your name has come up as a possible replacement for him. But you cannot obtain a command position without the recommendation of your commander." At these words, I laughed and said, "Terentianus would never recommend me!" When Sergius asked me to explain, I did not consider how my words might impact my life. I simply told him what was in my mind. "Terentianus is not a good Commander, for he does not care about his men. He obtained his present position through his family and political connections, and our success as a century is more in spite of him than anything else. He desires power above all things. He dislikes me because he perceives me as a threat. Let me give you an example: because he provides no training for the new recruits I have begun to do so when I am off duty. I am not doing this to pave the way for a better position for myself, but because these men were being killed and injured simply due to the fact that their skills were so limited. Instead of commending me for my initiative, Terentianus reprimanded me for doing this, claiming that I was usurping his authority. I am happy being a soldier, but would be happier if I had a commander who cared for his men more than his career!"

I went on in this vein for some time, until Paul walked into our conversation, and he continued, "John has helped improve the skills and morale of all the recruits. You can ask them yourself. Not only has Terentianus not recognized him for this, he deplores it, for he fears the men may become more loyal to John than to him. This is not the quality of a commander! Not only John has been treated unjustly! Whoever has stepped forward trying to do something for the other men, whether it be organizing trainings or planning new tactics before going to

---

[7] Trier, Germany, where Constantine had his headquarters during this time.

battle, whatever it is, Terentianus has seen this as a threat. I do not know which is worse, his indifference to his men or his plotting for a political position." It was with these and similar words that Paul and I told Sergius about our Commander.

I did not think of this conversation at all in the weeks that followed, but continued my duties as before. Much later, I learned of events that were occurring without my being aware. Terentianus had friends in the command who had told him that he was to be promoted shortly, and that the announcement would be made within days after the return of Sergius and his unit. When this did not take place, our Commander inquired repeatedly to discover what was causing the delay. At a certain point, I know not how, he learned that I was being considered for a command position, and that his promotion had been denied. Due to his deviousness, he suspected that I was at fault. He either found out or assumed that I had a conversation with Sergius about him, and that Paul was involved. I considered Sergius to be a friend; I still do not think that he betrayed me, but I still do not know how Terentianus learned of my words. In any event, our Commander went to great effort to tarnish my name and that of Paul. Through his powerful friends, he decided to rid himself of those he saw as a threat, and to punish us for thwarting his promotion. I knew none of this when orders came to report to his tent early one morning.

\*\*\*

Terentianus had a heavy bearing, being unaccustomed to any physical labor. When I entered his tent, he was lying down and did not rise to return my salute. "New orders for you. An important position in Alexandria. Goods are not arriving in Rome as they should. You will help to resolve the situation there. You will join a legion under Maxentius[8] and assist in the east. This is a great opportunity, a promotion for you. Your escort waits outside to accompany you south until you reach the ship that will take you there. You are not to stop on the way, for you will set sail in nine days," he said.

I was shocked and confused. I began to ask questions. "How did these orders come about? I have done nothing wrong."

He rose and said slowly, "No one has said that you did anything wrong. You have a new assignment. You are needed in Alexandria. The legion has called you. I am simply passing the orders to you. Others will be moved also."

I was still confused. I continued, "Can I at least stop in Rome to see my mother? May I delay my departure for several days here so I can ready myself?"

At this point he stood up and became angry. "No, no, no! These are your orders. Obey them." With these words he dismissed me.

As I left, I passed Paul who had also been called to the Commander. What was taking place here? Two soldiers approached me as my "escort," though it seemed I was being taken as a prisoner. Because I was esteemed, it was easy to convince them to allow me more time than the Commander had allotted, and we agreed to leave late in the day, and then to ride all night to make up the time. I went to my own tent and gathered my belongings, waiting to tell Paul what had happened. My "escort" implored me not to speak a word to the others, especially the new recruits, of my exile, for they would be punished for allowing me to stay in the camp for the rest of that day. Perhaps our Commander feared a rebellion. In any event, I agreed, for their sake.

\*\*\*

[8] At this time Maxentius was still recognized as Emperor in central and southern Italy, as well as Corsica, Sardinia, Sicily, and the African provinces.

Terentianus was less diplomatic with Paul, telling him that he had been a thorn in his side, accused him of supporting the murmuring against him, and that he too was to be transferred effective immediately.

"Where?" Paul asked in shock.

"There is a century in Gaul, the town of Arelate, that needs recruits; I have enlisted you there."

Paul said his mouth fell open. "Gaul? You are sending me to Gaul?" When the Commander did not reply, Paul continued, "Who else is receiving transfer orders?

Terentianus approached Paul and put his red face close to his and replied, "That is of no concern of yours, soldier!" and dismissed him.

Paul told me afterwards that he considered killing the Commander on that spot. "I had my sword, but I could have used my hands. My hatred was so intense that I would have finished him with one blow. But I restrained myself, using my head rather than my anger. So what did I do? I turned and left."

Perhaps Terentianus thought he could gain the loyalty of his men if he rid himself of those who made him feel inadequate. Perhaps he thought that he would rise sooner to the top commands if he squashed any opposition or competition. Perhaps it was revenge. I am not sure even now. I wondered whether he purposely sent Paul and me to different posts in the hope that it would cause us greater pain.

I remember that day as if it were occurring now; the ache and fear that all would be lost is still a wound in my heart. When Paul came to gather his things, I informed him of what was to take place. Instead of growing angry, he tried to comfort me as I was sitting on the ground, staring into nothingness, crippled in mind and movement. "Little brother, try not to be afraid; let us help one another as we have in battle. This is the same. Although I am afraid and saddened, I want to assure you that you will not be abandoned. I am more certain of this than I am of the sun rising tomorrow. I will not abandon you! I will become the best soldier in my century; I will take the command, then I will call you to come to my legion! I am sorry my orders are to report to Gaul. But you will not be alone. Do you believe me? John, if there are gods, if Mithras hears me now, may they not let all be lost. My brother, you know I would lay down my life for you, and you would do the same for me. The bond between us is greater than Terentianus can conceive. Are you with me, John?" I grabbed his arm and he mine, in the way of the legion. As I looked at him, I longed that the next moment would not arrive. As we finished packing our things, neither of us knew of any other words to say. If I had not been so stunned, I would have tried to comfort Paul before his departure, but I could say nothing.

Before long we were summoned from our tent and ordered to depart. I would not see Paul again for three years.

# Chapter 2: Exile

I had been trained as a soldier and had excelled in combat and strategy. I was therefore disappointed when I learned that my task in Egypt would be to guard the consignment of goods destined for Rome. For many generations, the Empire had relied on these shipments for the well being of the people, and disruptions in the past caused tensions and even riots. Grain was like gold to those living in the cities, and the land of the Pharaohs had produced enough of it for both its own inhabitants and Rome's. I understood the importance of guarding the transport to ensure that the shipments would arrive, because those living in Alexandria were sometimes unhappy in seeing their goods being carried off by Romans. I could not comprehend, however, why I had been given such a menial task simply because Terentianus was angered.

On the battlefield, I had always sought to turn any situation to my advantage, and I was resolved to apply the same tactic here. Although I was disappointed and angry at my lot, I would seek to learn new things, visit new places, and accumulate a new understanding of the world. I had no idea yet how I would accomplish this, but I kept this resolution firm in my mind as we approached this mysterious place.

When we arrived in Alexandria, I was astounded, for I never knew that such a beautiful city could be built by men. We first glimpsed it at night as we approached the harbor, guided by the

*Pharos* lighthouse.[9] There were perhaps fifty other men on board who spent hours that night, marveling over the light which guided us. The city could be seen in the background, gleaming white in the full moon. As dawn approached the entire landscape took on a pink hue, and we pushed further into the harbor where twenty other soldiers and I disembarked.

Alexandria had a long history of turmoil ever since it became a Roman province. The city was punished after the death of Cleopatra; its citizens had rioted time and again, and some emperors, such as Diocletian, had treated the Alexandrians with harshness.[10] At this time, however, there was relative peace.

\*\*\*

As I walked with the other new arrivals through the streets, I could hear Latin, Hebrew, Greek, and Persian spoken. It was truly a city in which the world met. I had never been in any place that could compare. I had heard stories of Rome, but had never been there. Alexandria seemed to have been made by the gods, I thought to myself.

My group was met by a messenger who brought me and the others to the place where our men were to be stationed. The new century to which I belonged had various tasks throughout the city; only a small number of us were assigned to guard duty at the port.

I was dismayed when I found that I had been assigned with the new recruits, the *tirones*, who had no experience in battle at all. This was too much, I thought, as I made my way to my new

---

[9] The *Pharos* was begun about 290 B.C.E. It was considered one of the seven wonders of the ancient world, due to its beauty and technology. Its light could be seen up to fifty kilometers off shore, guiding ships into the harbor of Alexandria.

[10] During his reign of 284-305 C.E., Diocletian devastated the administrative unity of Egypt by dividing it into three provinces. He also unleashed a brutal persecution of Christians, beginning in Alexandria, blaming the new religion for resistance to Roman rule.

commander. Although I greeted him with respect, he looked at me with suspicion. I asked him why I was with the *tirones*; I had been in the legion for years, and had much battle experience. He approached me and replied, "Your place is with the new recruits. With your orders of transfer came word that you can be troublesome, insubordinate, and disloyal toward those in command. I have been instructed to grant you no privileges, but to treat you as a *tiro* and train you as one. You will be a new soldier, and will not breed disloyalty as you did in Germania. Dismissed," he said, before I could respond. The hatred of Terentianus had followed me here.

\*\*\*

After several weeks, my daily duties developed into a mindless routine. Every day I was to stand guard at the docks. Such a task soon bored me, but I felt helpless to change my situation. I recalled my resolution to use this time to my advantage. Therefore, every day when I finished my duties, I began my own training and battle practice so that I would not be at a disadvantage should I be called onto the field. I maintained my physical condition and practiced with my weapons daily. This occupied the hours when I was not fulfilling my duty, but my spirit grew restless. I returned to honoring the god Mithras as I had done sporadically in Germania, along with many in my century. The courage inspired by the cult drew many in the various legions to this worship. My spirit longed for more than the mere observance of precepts, so I decided to walk more deeply in the Mithraic path. Though I had not yet been initiated,[11] I immersed myself into the world of this god.

I went to a Mithraeum in Alexandria which was frequented by others in my legion and sought out instruction. In the weeks

---

[11] The Mithraic initiation consisted of a formal commitment in the presence of the community. To be accepted, the initiate would have to successfully pass through various ordeals.

that followed, I was taught the story of the god. The Mithraic priest told us that Mithras allied himself to the sun and planned to slay the bull, because it was the first creature ever created. Under the command of the sun, he took the animal and dragged it into a cave where he slew it. This was not a tragedy, for from the dead animal the world sprang into being.

It was said that Mithras came from the east; some claimed that he proceeded from Rome's enemies, the Persians, but I would not believe this. [12] During his life, the god practiced control of his passions, sacrifice for what is good, and renunciation of every evil. He never embraced another in a carnal way, sacrificing his own desires to give life to the world. He encouraged his followers to form a brotherhood in order to fight against evil in this life so as to find goodness in the next. The priest instructed us that Mithras was the mediator between heaven and earth who would judge all at the end of time. The dead would rise again in the body, and light would finally triumph over darkness. In the meantime, Mithras would continue to protect his faithful from above.

Many, including myself, were drawn to this cult because we knew that we could not subdue others until we learned how to master ourselves. This was the way of the god: to learn to subject what is lower in oneself to what is higher. The passions were to be subjected to the mind, emotion guided by reason. By walking this path, we would grow in strength and endurance, and we would attain life in the beyond.

The Mithraeum that I frequented was, like most, a cave with two raised areas along the length of the room. Here the initiates sat and partook of the mysteries. There was little light within; lamps were used because the proceedings were secret and were not to be exposed to the light of day. There was an empty pool between the two benches where the blood of a sacrificed bull would flow. At the forefront, in the center, was the stone figure

---

[12] Lactantius Placidus, *Comm. in Stat. Theb.* 1.719-20.

of Mithras, about to plunge the knife into the neck of the bull. In the depiction, however, the god looks away because he is receiving his instructions to kill the animal from another god, the Sun. I would learn that Mithras obeyed not his own will, but that of the all powerful Sun, just as his followers must learn to obey the will of the gods.

On the sides of the Mithraeum were other carved figures telling the story of Mithras: his birth from a rock, having his origins from the earth.[13] That first day I entered into that cool place, shielded from the hot Alexandrian sun. I sat down and looked closely at the story of the god told in stone along the walls. To my right was an icon in which Mithras was shooting an arrow at a rock from which water gushed forth as a source of fertility and purity. I would learn that much water would be used in the mysteries to wash what was unclean from inside and out. To my left, toward the front of the cave, was another figure of Mithras carrying a flame. There was a lamp burning before this figure. Here too, I would be instructed that the fire symbolized the sun which was a god, but also a power which abides within men. If the god was honored, and the course of the sun through the day and seasons was respected, then men would be happy and prosper. In the middle of the wall on my left was a figure of Mithras standing in front of the sun, which means he was divine. The most important figure, as I said, is that of Mithras killing the bull which was in the front center, with several lamps under and around it. We would be instructed that this killing was an act of courage, obedience, and love, and that from it, all of nature sprang. In this way Mithras became the savior and friend of man.

\*\*\*

"Are you ready to begin the road to initiation?" the Mithraic priest asked me after I had been frequenting the rites for several

---

[13] Commodianus, *Instructiones*. 1.13.

months. This process of initiation consisted of seven steps, corresponding to the seven planetary gods. The first step had as its symbol the crow, because it is from this creature that the divinity of the sun spoke, instructing Mithras to slay the bull, and so bring forth the life of the god. The crow, I was also taught, is the sign of death; this path would lead to the slaying of my old self. The planetary god who watched over those who began this journey was Mercury.[14]

"Yes," I replied. Why I began this intense following of this god, I can only explain now in terms of being deprived of those things that gave my life meaning in the past. I was eager to find a way to be happy here and to make progress on many levels. I was a soldier, and as such, I always sought to better myself.

In the weeks that followed I was instructed on the meaning of faith in the god, and it was explained to me as a type of re-birth. When I stepped forward at the initiation ceremony I was asked a series of questions by the head priest, called the *pater patrum*,[15] in order to measure my worthiness. After this I was washed with water so that I might leave all evil behind. A torch was then handed to me, symbolizing the Sun god which spoke to Mithras. Following this, the members embraced me.

I had a new task: any evil that I had done in the past was to remain dead to me. I was called to begin a new life in following the god. Besides this, I was to bring the message of Mithras into the world by the way that I lived, just as the crow brought the message to the god, bringing about the slaying of the bull, and so the new world. I was called to treat others with respect and to put into practice the teachings that the priest would impart to me.

For several months I balanced my duties at the dock, my battle practice, and attending the Mithraic mysteries. I sought to live what I was taught, which was fairly easy, because I kept so much to myself that I quarreled with no one.

---

[14] Origen, *Contra Celsum*, 6.22, and Jerome, *Epistle* 107.2.
[15] *Pater patrum* can be translated as "father of fathers."

Besides the rite of acceptance, there were trials of strength and endurance to undergo if one was to travel along this path.[16] Their exact nature was secret, so I did not know what to expect when I was asked to appear at the Mithraeum the next day at an appointed hour. The *pater patrum* was present, as well as others, and he placed a blindfold around my head. I was then led to another room, at which time I was instructed, "Fight not to free yourself, but await the liberation of the god." At this point, my hands were tied behind my back, and I was led forward. "Proceed three paces," I was instructed, and as I did so I lost my balance and suddenly fell into a cistern filled with extremely cold water. I struggled to rise above the water, spitting it out, and in a panic. I then discovered that the depth came only to my shoulders, and I could stand and breathe sufficiently. This was a test, I thought to myself, that I was determined to pass successfully. Once I had my bearings I stood in that water and waited to be freed. No one stepped forward to release me, and consequently I suffered greatly from the cold. I refused to manifest my discomfort as I clenched my teeth so as to stop their chattering and widened my stance so as to face the enemy, which was the cold, and my own wish to recoil against it. I waited and waited, still as a soldier awaiting orders to charge forth. After a long time, another jumped into the water with me, cut my hands free, and pulled me out. All present congratulated me. I had passed this test.

There were more quiet times when I would find myself before the altar of Mithras alone. I would try to think of only the courageous deeds of the god, but so often my mind would wander to where my heart dwelt. As the faces of those I loved came to haunt me, I would ask the god to watch over them, especially Paul, until I would see them once again.

"Are you ready to prove your worthiness once more?" the

---

[16] Some sources claim there were as many as eight ordeals to be overcome by the initiates. Psuedo-Nonnus, Comm. *in Greg. Nazian. Or.* 4. 70.

priest asked me some weeks later.

I stood and said, "Yes."

He instructed me to gather all of my gear, including my sword and shield, and to meet at the Mithraeum the next day. When I did so, I was instructed, "You are to carry only the food and water which will be given to you now. You are to march east until the moon has risen and then has gone. You will then turn and march back. It will then be morning, and you will report to the dock for your duties." This ordeal truly made me angry, but I accepted the challenge and did as I was instructed. The next day the priest approached me once again and said I would be required to undergo the same ordeal on the following night. Three times he asked me to do so within a five day period. I was exhausted. On my return that third time, as he was waiting for me in front of the garrison, I walked past him and threw my sword down and tossed my helmet after it. I was furious. He approached me and said, "The god did not only endure suffering, but he mastered himself. In the same way, it is only when you master your anger that you will be free of what binds you to your old life." With this he left.

I continued this path for many months, being subjected to other trials, until one day, while resting in the calm and darkness of the Mithraeum, the priest approached me and said, "I believe you are ready for the second level." I looked up at him and nodded.

\*\*\*

The second stage had as its symbol the Nymph, which was symbolized by the serpent consuming the blood of the bull slain by Mithras. Venus would watch over those who pursued this way, helping them seek purification through this blood. Thus I was instructed. When the ceremony came for me to make this step, I remember being admitted to the Mithraeum covered in a yellow veil. I was led by the hand, being unable to see. When the veil was removed I was told, "Now you are a full member of this Mithraeum. You must learn to subdue yourself before you can subdue others." Those who embraced this step were required to be entirely celibate until the next level. This I sought to do with all my strength.

The ordeals associated with this stage were also in place to help one overcome his own fears, and to build his endurance. I was tested with fire, hunger, thirst, and fatigue. Once I was asked to march until told to stop by a representative of the Mithraeum. I marched through the morning, afternoon, and evening. I kept marching in the same direction, determined to manifest no fatigue. The order to stop only came the next morning, after marching all night. Though this was difficult, it was the test with fire that I recall most vividly, for I was asked to trust the *pater* of the Mithraeum with my very eyesight as he ordered the approach of one who had a red hot iron. When he was several feet away from me, he was ordered to brand me on the forehead with the iron; I did not withdraw, but continued to gaze into the eyes of the would-be brander. As he approached further, I showed neither fear nor recoiling, and as he brought the iron to my eyes I did not permit myself to blink. Before he could burn my flesh, another approached and pulled him back. I had passed the ordeal.

\*\*\*

After nearly half a year, without notice, the *pater* approached me and said, "You are ready." With these words I entered into the third sphere. This was the stage at which I had aimed, for it was that of the *miles*, or soldiers. At this stage we were asked to honor Mars as our patron. The instruction to those taking this step took place in the Mithraeum before the figure of the scorpion, which stings the testicles of the bull as it is dying under the strike of Mithras. It was explained to us that just as the scorpion was able to take the virility of the dying bull, so we were to do the same from the god himself, becoming courageous, strong, and certain of victory.

The rites involved with this mystery were so secret that we were threatened with death should we ever reveal them. But I write of them here, for I fear not the wrath of Mithras.

This is what took place: I found myself in darkness, kneeling before the Mithraic *pater*, or priest. I offered him reverence as he anointed my head. I was then handed a sword and led to a room, illuminated with only one lamp, in which a crown was placed on a table with an armed soldier standing in front of it. My task would be to either subdue him, or be subdued; if I succeeded, the crown would be mine. If I failed, I would not be accepted into the third rank.

The soldier at hand was unknown to me. Taller than I, and with muscles that rivaled those of Hercules, he was an intimidating figure. I was seasoned by combat, however, and showed no misgiving or hesitation as I leapt forward to battle this man. He was taken by surprise by my swiftness as I landed my sword heavily on his shield and then faced him, just as ferocious as he was. It took him but a moment to gather himself and attempt to land his sword, but I was too swift; I ducked, then caught him from behind. My experience and practice these past months paid off as I kept him continuously off guard. My task was not to kill him, or even to wound him, but simply to subdue him. He was a courageous man who would not give up easily. He turned and landed his sword once, twice, then a third time on my shield, numbing my hand and arm, but I did not lose my balance or composure. I quickly swung back and forced him to back up, losing his balance for an instant, which I took advantage of. I jumped forward and thrust my sword against his breast plate, then swiftly up toward his throat. He grew fearful and dropped his shield. All was over. I was now ready to enter the third rank.

\*\*\*

I was instructed that, in the third level of the mysteries, I was never to seek my own glory, but only that of Mithras. I would show my willingness to do so in the rite which would mark this beginning. I was led into the Mithraeum with hands tied behind my back, stripped of most of my clothes. The priest waited for me, and I knelt before him. At this point, a man with a sword appeared, and on its tip was a crown which he placed on my head. He stepped behind me and slashed my bindings. I removed the crown and placed it on my shoulder, then cried, "Only Mithras is my crown!" At this point, a Phrygian hat was placed on my head in place of the crown. It is the same hat that the god wore when he slew the bull.[17]

I was then led out to the central part of the Mithraeum where others who were at some stage of initiation were gathered. Below the altar of the god were large bowls filled with blood. With the priest in the middle, and all of us lined up on both sides, he explained to us, "Behold the blood from which new life comes into the world. You are also cleansed by water and reborn in the blood of the bull which was slain. Partake of the mercy and strength of Mithras from whom all life flows." With these words, we were anointed with the blood on our foreheads, shoulders, and hands. The rest of the blood was then poured into two gutters on each side, made to flow the length of that place where we were gathered. Water was then brought in, and we all washed ourselves and cleansed the floor and gutters of any remaining blood.[18] This completed, the priest said, "Come, let us feast in the presence of the god." He bade us to be seated along the sides.

At the sacred banquet we ate of the roasted bull, and then ate of the bread and water offerings.[19] There were about twenty-five of us who partook, but I was the only one present from my cohort. I asked Mithras to make me courageous and wise, after his example.

---

[17] Tertullian, *De Corona* 15.

[18] Tertullian *De Praecriptione heareticorum*, 40. 3-4

[19] Justin Martyr, *1 Apology*, 66.

Over the next months I devoted myself to fulfilling this third stage, especially to master my fear and anger. The *pater* indicated to me what the ordeal would be that I must pass through. "You are angry at being sent to Alexandria, angry at being separated from your companions and family, angry at your former Commander. Your resentment is what keeps you from moving forward on this road you have begun. You must wash yourself of the past so that you can follow the god in this place, for it is only when you no longer mind being here that the god will permit you to leave. You are holding yourself back. You must free yourself. That is your task." With these words he dismissed me.

How to fulfill the words of the priest was not yet clear to me, but I was determined to discover their meaning.

I continued to honor the god in all the other ways, setting aside that first day of every week dedicated to the sun, and celebrating with great feasting on his day in December when the sun would begin to overcome death and darkness. I asked Mithras daily to protect those that I loved, to help me grow in courage, and to have the strength to subdue that resentment which simmered in my heart.

\*\*\*

There were seven steps in all, in order for one to belong fully to the god, and it can take many years to succeed in all of them. I did not continue beyond *miles*, for my time in Egypt would come to a close, and my devotion to the god would eventually lessen. For now, much of my world revolved around the Mithraeum.

Though my devotion to Mithras had not been as intense in Germania as it was in Egypt, in Germania I enjoyed the camaraderie which honoring the god generated. Participating in the rites increased the sense of brotherhood in the legion, and that is why it was encouraged. This was lacking in Alexandria. My commitment was strong, but the brotherhood was absent, I know not why. Perhaps it was my loneliness which intensified my devotion to the god and kept me apart from others. Perhaps it was my anger. I was isolated from other garrisons, and I saw the new recruits, the *tirones,* as children with whom I had nothing in common. My present Commander seemed better than Terentianus, but he was a distant figure with whom I had no association.

I tried to fill my mind and my heart with my dedication to the god, but despite my efforts, I always felt alone. Paul had become my family, Crispinianus and Crispus my brothers, and I remained attached to Fulvia, and to my mother. I made a great effort to deaden these feelings, seeking in the mystery rites a sort of black peace in which I would not be disturbed by anything. I sought tranquility in emptiness, trying to forget, trying not to think of the past, trying to focus on nothingness. I was not always successful. It was as if my body and heart were at war, and no matter how hard I tried to bring my heart back, it somehow always slipped away again, leaving me alone.

\*\*\*

It was during this time that I often wondered if the gods had some plan for my being in the land of the Pharaohs. Was there some purpose, something that I was to learn or discover while here, besides my following of Mithras? These were my thoughts when the most irritating orders arrived at the docks one day; due to insufficient workers and an overabundance of goods needing to be shipped out, we were to put away our tasks as soldiers and become dock workers. We were to load the ships until the transport had caught up with the backlog of goods. It was summer, which made the work more difficult, but I did not mind the physical labor. What I resented was the dishonor; it was like being demoted once again. I felt that I had not fought to protect the borders of the Empire in Germania, only to be subjected to this humiliation. I suppressed my irritation, for I had no recourse. Perhaps, I thought, this was also a test, that I might master my anger.

The orders were vague, so I stepped forward and organized the men in the fairest way possible. Due to the hot weather, the work was done only in the early morning and the evening. This prolonged the task, but was necessary because we Romans were not accustomed to the heat of Alexandria. I worked closer with the men than before and was impressed by their good will. In fact, they did not seem to mind the labor; their willingness to complete the task every day made my resentment diminish as time passed. After a fortnight, the backlog had been reduced, and the shipping was able to return to its normal pace. We were able to return to our normal duties.

***

One evening after our task was complete, our regiment was given release time, and I went to an inn where I met an Egyptian woman.

"You do not scorn Romans like most do," I said to her, after she had filled my glass with wine a second time.

"I leave it to the gods to judge between men," she replied. "What benefit is it to me if I treat you as less because you are fulfilling what you must do, as am I here. My family has owned this inn for three generations, and all who enter are treated with respect."

"What is your name?" I asked.

"Merytre," she replied.

"I am John. May I come here again and speak with you?" She laughed.

"Our door is always open, Roman John. May the gods watch over your steps," she said as she turned away.

In Alexandria I had no one who would hear my inner thoughts. I was looking for companionship, so the very next night I found myself at the inn once more.

"Merytre," I asked, "what is the meaning of the monuments

of stone?" She sat down at my table across from me and looked at me intensely.

"You are a Roman. What do you think?" I sensed hostility in her eyes, but I said nothing. She continued, "You conquer the world without even knowing what it is you are subduing." I continued to gaze at her, and she slowly realized that I was not challenging her, nor was I representing the Empire; I was simply a man with a question. She relaxed a bit and began, "Our ancestors built the pyramids to honor our Pharaohs, but also to honor our god Aten, for it is the sun that gives life to all. Our leaders are buried there with all that they need to pass from this life to the next. So in these monuments is enshrined our belief in the power of the gods and in the life that comes after."

I reflected, then asked, "Is this what *you* hold to be true, Merytre?" She laughed as she rose.

"You ask me difficult questions, Roman. Let us think of these things and speak again," and she left.

Night after night I was at the inn as our friendship and conversation grew. "My father looks at me strangely because I spend time with a Roman," she said one evening.

"How does that make you feel?" I asked.

"It makes me feel nothing," she replied. "I judge no one, as he taught me."

Because there were few at the inn that evening I proceeded to question her about her gods. "I also honor the sun god, but we call him Mithras. Last night you told me that your gods help you after death. But how do they help you through life? Do they make any difference in the way that you live?"

She paused and thought for what seemed a long time. "Those of the royal line instituted the official worship of the gods, and you see our many priests making offerings at the temples to honor them. But I am not of royal blood. I am the daughter of an innkeeper. To me, these gods have meaning only at the great festivals. My family honors our own gods in our home. My mother had my father build an altar where we honor Bes and

Taweret, as well as our ancestors. Many families like ours honor these more humble gods who are good hearted and watch over us." I marveled at how similar her ways were to Romans, but before I could ask Merytre if she thought so also, she arose again to help her father.

Several evenings later, I found myself back at the inn; I had been thinking of our previous words, so I asked her, "Merytre, you tell me that your gods watch over you in this life and guide you to a new life in the next. Do you serve them out of fear, because without them, terrible things may happen?"

She laughed, as she often did, and then became quiet as she reflected. "Roman, you always ask me such complex questions!" She smiled and left the table to serve others. A short while later, she returned and said, "Our duties are to honor the gods and our dead, to obey our rulers, and to fulfill our responsibilities."

Before she left again, I replied, "It is the same for us. But for you, Merytre, is that enough? Is that what your gods ask of you, simply your duty? Is that why they have put us here, to do our duty, then to die to be with those gods who have required so much, yet have given so little?"

She replied, "Oh no, Roman, it is not enough. But what else is there?" and she left again to serve the other guests.

I became a frequent visitor, and I often pressed Merytre for answers, because I sought them for myself. Few Egyptians neglected honoring the gods, and I kept seeking the reason why. Fear? Custom? Or did they understand something that I did not?

I was honoring the gods and disciplining myself, and yet my spirit was empty. This perplexed me, for I had been taught that happiness is the reward for those who do what is right.

I had almost succeeded in deadening myself to any pain until I received a letter from my sister. Although I had received correspondence from her and Paul before, this time I was deeply affected. Feelings welled up inside of me as I read her words.

*My dear brother,*

*Those who love you think of you often and have not stopped striving to obtain your return among us. Your being exiled in Egypt is unjust, and we have begun to work quietly on your behalf. My husband has some contacts that will help. The affairs in the Empire are changing quickly, and we are hopeful this will mean your return. I am sure Paul will tell you more. Mother is well. I am with child, and Gaius and I are very happy.*

*Fulvia*

In Germania, although I was far from my sister, I felt that I was part of the events which enveloped her life. When she had our mother move into her home with her husband, we had made this decision together. Now it was as if I were seeing her life pass me by through a small hole in the wall. I could only observe part of what was on the other side, but could not climb over. This would have to be enough, I told myself. I heard from Fulvia every twenty five to thirty days, and from Paul about every fifteen days. Their letters gave me both joy and sorrow.

*My brother,*

*As always, I write you to assure you that I always carry you in my heart. Your pain is mine, as is your joy. I do believe the gods will favor us with your return, for they will surely undo what is unjust. Fear not. I am working to gain the respect of my Commander, for this will give me his ear, which I will then use for your benefit.*

*Paul*

It was especially for Paul that my heart languished, for we

were companions in affection as well as battle. In this place, I was becoming the stern and hard person I had been when I first entered the legion. Perhaps I would end up as hard as that rock from which it was said that Mithras was born. It was as if part of me was slipping away, and I did not know how to stop it. Perhaps it was better this way.

***

After some months, war was in the air. Even before the reports arrived, I could sense it. It was said that the Romans hated Maxentius, feeling that he levied many taxes which were not then used for the benefit of the people. He was known to be cruel to his own people, using his power only for his own advantage. [20] His father had betrayed him and support for Maxentius among his own military was wavering. Because he was unsure of the allegiance of the legions in the east, it was unlikely that we would be called for duty any time soon. There was much confusion as to where one should place one's loyalty. It was said that the only ones Maxentius could trust were the Praetorians, and he had thousands of them. I had no respect for the Praetorians, for they were mindless men who only understood orders from above.

The news had reached us that Constantine, knowing that Maxentius was vulnerable, had assembled a great mass of men in Gaul and was preparing to march south to Rome. I knew this because the garrison of Paul in Arelate was near that very place where this army was being prepared.

I had a letter from Paul.

*Brother,*

*I implored my Commander to release me so that I*

---

[20] Eusebius, *Vita Constantinae*, 35.

*might march to Rome also, and participate in the conquest of our Emperor. The adventure of the battle will be without precedent. I would say that I wish you were here to accompany me, but my Commander has refused all of my requests and threatened me with punishment should I ask him again. It seems that our garrison must remain here to quell any uprisings that may occur once that battle has begun. It is also claimed that the Strike Force which will march south has received particular training for this battle, and their commanders do not want to receive centuries that they do not know. It is also a question of loyalty; it seems all sides fear just who might be faithful to whom when the fighting erupts. So here I stay, on the side, just as we would go to the games and watch, not participating.*

*I am hopeful that these changing events will not only be good for the Empire, but will bring you back here where you belong.*

*I have heard from your sister; she is leaving Rome until these things pass and their outcome is sure. She said she will keep me informed of her whereabouts. If you do not hear from her during this period, do not be distressed.*

*I embrace you.*

*Paul*

This was the last communication that reached me for several months, but the events which followed shook the Empire and made us all wonder what changes these events would bring. Constantine did indeed go to battle with Maxentius outside of Rome; the latter lost his life, his soldiers lost their leader, and

Constantine triumphed.[21] Now he ruled almost half the Empire. He is currently establishing his own authority in Rome. There were changes in the legion also; he dissolved the Praetorian completely because he could not be sure of their loyalty. Some centuries were moved, and many commanders were replaced.

Finally, a communication from Paul arrived.

*Brother,*

*Your sister is well and has returned to Rome. The changes in the Empire have now arrived here in Arlete. I have received orders to report to Rome with my garrison. Crispus and Crispinianus have notified me that they are to report to Ostia. The only one who is still to receive orders to come here is you. I am sure that will change soon. The Empire is changing. I dare not write more.*

*Paul*

\*\*\*

Events seemed to move with increasing speed: the Empire in the west was now one, there were new agreements of cooperation between Constantine and Licinius as to how to create a greater unity among the provinces, and various legions were receiving new orders. I wondered what commands might arrive in Alexandria. Then, another letter from Paul arrived.

*John,*

*I have now been in Rome for almost three weeks. I have seen your sister on several occasions. I am sorry*

---

[21] The battle of the Milvian Bridge outside of Rome occurred in 312. C.E. Eusebius, *Vita Constantinae*, 38.

*about the illness of your mother. Fulvia assures me that all will be well. I was with Crispus and Crispinianus last night; they too are happy to be near Rome, and we are content to be united. They have become formidable soldiers, having increased in strength and skill.*

*I have not been made a commander, but I have some friends with authority to whom I have already spoken of you. Fulvia said that her husband is also acting on your behalf. Have patience.*

*I embrace you.*

*Paul*

I was consoled by the letter from Paul with the exception of the part about my mother. I realized that Fulvia was keeping things from me. Was it to shield me from distress? I wrote to her and Paul, imploring them to keep me informed of any developments regarding my mother or any other matter. Though I would have to wait for weeks for detailed news, only in this way could I feel that my life was not completely separate from theirs. Because I did not trust Fulvia to tell me all, I wrote to Paul asking him to give me a complete account of matters regarding my mother.

I grew despondent because I was separated from my ill mother, and I was cut off from the exciting changes sweeping through the Empire. I grew angrier at Terentianus, and I was consoled by the thought that his envy and hunger for power would eventually destroy him. But I did not realize what my hatred for him and my anger at my predicament were doing to me. I withdrew from others in my unit even more and grew deaf to the words of the *pater* at the Mithraeum.

\*\*\*

I sought out Merytre as a companion with whom I could

share my feelings and questions, and she took pleasure in giving me the perspective of her people on whatever I posed to her. I always pushed her to give me her opinion and not simply what she had been told.

On one occasion she said to me, "It seems to me, John, that if you allow your hatred for your Commander to master you, your anger at being here will blind you, then you will miss the very thing the gods are trying to show you in bringing you to this place." I smiled, for it was as if the priest at the Mithraeum had told her what to say.

But then I broke in: "And what is it that I am supposed to learn here?"

She laughed and replied "I do not know what the gods have planned for you John, but you will never know either if you do not begin to open your eyes and stop thinking of this as a punishment. You know the tale of Odysseus of the Greeks. He was not permitted to return home until he learned that which the gods had ordained for him. Your life is like that. Do not close yourself in hate, for it is only yourself you will destroy. Besides this, you will be a very unpleasant companion." With these words she laughed, rose, and left.

On the following evenings we discussed why the gods permit hardship to those who follow them faithfully.

"You search for justice and find that it is fleeting. You seek love, and it also either slips away or does not satisfy!" I told her one evening.

She replied in her thoughtful manner, "The gods have put us in this world as one great question. We grasp on to this thing or that person as if they were the answers we sought. But the answers pale. The question within us remains."

One evening Merytre offered to take me on a tour through her city on the condition that I dispense with my uniform and dress as a Greek. I agreed. We met when the moon was full and the entire city was illuminated by a silvery glow. Alexandria is gleaming white when the sun is high due to the stone used in its construction, but I had never noticed its mysteriousness until that night with Merytre. "It is said that the city was more beautiful before the time of the Romans," she began, "because the royal families kept Alexandria in repair. We have had earthquakes which have damaged the royal palace. But it is still extraordinary. It is said that the spirit of Cleopatra still dwells there. You will see. Come." Because it was late there were few about. She led as I followed her on that peaceful night through the narrow streets and alleys, toward the harbor. We turned a corner and entered a great square paved with white stone, and there stood the palace right on the shore. The waters were lapping up against its outer wall, and part of its citadel had crumbled and fallen. It glowed in the moonlight, for it was made of that same Alexandrian stone. "Now Roman military officers use the royal apartments for offices, where once Cleopatra and Marc Antony plotted their strategies against Augustus and his men," and she laughed. I stood for a while and took in the scene. In the highest windows there was flickering light and sea gulls flying back and forth, as if to peer inside. There was an overgrown garden below which extended to the water. Off shore were small boats with fisherman and lamps. "Do you feel her?" Merytre asked. "She would come here to swim at night in secret when the worries of the kingdom were too much. She would watch over these waters for the return of Julius Caesar and Marc Anthony. Listen," she said, as we paused and listened to the waves as the moon reflected a long path over the water. She beckoned me over to the palace. "Place your hand here," she said, as she touched the white stone wall. "When I was a little girl, I would come here and place my hand on these stones. Then I would listen. It was as if I could hear the stones speak, or rather the voices of those who had lived within these walls. I would especially hear Cleopatra, and her laugh. Try to listen," she said, and I did let my imagination carry me as hers did. "I hope you do not think that I have lost my reason, John. But I want to show you Alexandria through the eyes of the people. I want you to hear the voice of the city, just as every true Alexandrian can hear." We paused for a long while as the waves lapped the side of the palace, the stars came out, and the moon shone. I kept my hand on the cool stone wall as we stood in silence. Suddenly Merytre took my hand and said, "Come," and we walked out of the square.

Merytre turned to me and continued, "Now we are approaching what has been the center of learning in Alexandria for hundreds of years. This is called the *Mouseion*.[22] It was here that all the knowledge of the world was kept in the great library. Much of it was lost when it was burned at the time of your Julius Caesar." I looked at the white walls and pillars in the pale light. It was in the style of several great temples, side by side.

"But the buildings look whole. The library is not destroyed."

Merytre smiled and replied "The *Mouseion* was rebuilt here, for not all was lost. Beside it you see the academy in which scholars devote their lives to the study of the texts. The collections are not as vast as before, but here are preserved writings so ancient that they exist nowhere else. For this reason, scholars come from long distances to stay here a while and read and copy these texts. It is sad to see how far the collection has fallen. It is said that some have crumbled into dust and others have been corrupted due to neglect. We have no way to support this vast *Mouseion* as the Ptolemies once did. We Alexandrians cannot even enter here without the permission of the Roman magistrate. So here we stand, at this gate."

At these words she paused, and we walked towards the front of the building. We could see the great bronze doors between the pillars of white stone. She began again, "Those who enter here can discover worlds which we have not even dreamed of." We

---

[22] The *Mouseion* or Museum was started by Ptolemy I Soter in about 300 B.C.E. His goal was to collect all the writings of the world. At its peak, the *Mouseion* housed 600,000 to 700,000 works. The complex consisted of the Great Library, classrooms, and lecture halls. It declined and was ultimately destroyed in the late fourth century C.E.

remained and looked at the building through an outer gate for some time. There was a garden around a pool, behind which the *Mouseion* stood, constructed of that Alexandrian, glowing white stone. There were many columns along the entire side of the main building, supporting a long balcony above. There were many pairs of large windows on the upper floor with decorative carvings between each pair. All the windows were dark, and there was silence. As I gazed into the garden, I gradually made out the figure of a man sitting near the pool. I could not see his face, only his clothes, because he was dressed in white which reflected the moonlight. He was still, only occasionally shifting his position slightly. There he sat, gazing at the pool. For many minutes we stood there, and I looked upon him and wondered what his thoughts were.

We wandered back to the harbor and looked at that marvel called the *Pharos.* "For centuries this light has been guiding ships safely through dangers. It is the same with Alexandria. Through our history and our learning, we too have been a *Pharos* to many others, both within our land and far away. Now it is Rome that guides the world, but I hope that she learns from our history, from our scholars, so that our legacy will continue. Would that I could take you to our other monuments to the south, for there you would see the wonders of the pyramids and the beauty of our temples! Recall the man in the garden at the *Mouseion.* He *is* Alexandria. You ask me how and why we honor our gods. What I have shown you is the answer. It is in our stones, walls, our waves and wind, our scholars and innkeepers. This is the answer to your question. Yes, Roman John, Alexandria has taught many people how to live, perhaps even you Romans, if you would listen and learn, and not only conquer and subdue."

She paused, and I started in, "Merytre, I understand your anger at Rome. I would feel the same if I were in your place. But do not detest all Romans."

"John," she interrupted, "I do not detest you. You are

different."

"I am the same as the others. Just as you must rise and clean the inn and prepare the meals and feed your guests, so I must rise and accomplish my duties so as to succeed in being faithful to the path the gods have laid out for me. My companions in my garrison must do the same. Are we so dissimilar, then?" Merytre smiled.

"Perhaps not so much."

We were standing against a low stone wall with the *Pharos* behind us and the full moon now high in the sky. We could once again hear the waters lapping below.

"Roman John," she began, "why do you inquire so much concerning our gods and how we honor them?"

I reflected on my reasons before I replied, "I wondered how *you* honor your gods, not all of Egypt, so that I might learn what is lacking in my fidelity." We had spoken many times, and by now Merytre could see the meaning through my words.

"I recall what you said to me one night at the inn, for you wondered how one could fulfill one's duty to the gods, and yet still be abandoned by them, as you feel here. I understand what you say, Roman John, and I have thought about this many times since that night. Perhaps the gods reveal to us our duty alone. Perhaps we are only shown how to live with honor." She paused at this, then continued, "My father has contracted my marriage many years past, and I have not met the one I shall marry. I will probably not meet him until the day we wed, for his family lives far from Alexandria. I will travel to his land, marry him, and live far from my home for the rest of my days. It is my duty to do so, and I accept it at the hands of our families, and from the gods. But will I be happy? I can only do my duty. I cannot foresee happiness. Perhaps this is the way the gods have planned out our lives."

I replied to her, "Perhaps we are simply meant to do our duty, to others as well as the gods, and perhaps happiness is not for all, but simply for a few." At this we grew silent and looked out over the waves.

These words were difficult, but I could not discount them. Since the moment of my arrival, I had longed to be in Rome with Paul and Fulvia and the others whom I loved. I was convinced that I could only be happy if I left this place to be with them. Perhaps that will not be the road chosen for me by the gods. Perhaps I will stay here my entire life. Or perhaps I will return to Rome only to find there all manner of tribulations, and instead of happiness, will find only sorrow. I knew not the answer to these questions, but it consoled me to have found one who shared them.

"My father will grow suspicious if I do not return now. You must leave me here, and we'll go our separate ways. I have enjoyed our time. Peace." Before I had a chance to reply she had turned, covered her head, and ran down the side street.

I continued to see Merytre at the inn, for both our friendship and our conversations deepened. She was careful not to neglect her duties, but came to my table when she could. We spoke of courage and honor as well as happiness and love. We both tried to understand how the gods sometimes honored, and other times ignored, men's hearts. We continued in this way for several weeks until one evening, when I entered, I noted immediately that she seemed upset. I also noticed that her father was watching me intently. When it came time for me to be served, he approached my table. He allowed his daughter to serve other tables, but not mine. I surmised he was wary of our friendship. Merytre said that no one was judged who came to this inn, but I could see that in his eyes I was simply a Roman, a customer, and an enemy. A few days later Merytre managed to approach my table while her father was distracted. "My father has forbidden me to speak with you. He believes in the old ways. Do not come to the inn for a time. Without your face burning in his mind, perhaps he will forget. I will send word when he has calmed. It is better not to speak of this here," she said, as she turned when her father approached.

With no one to share my thoughts with in this strange land, I rededicated myself to only my duties. In this way I could deafen myself so as not to be disturbed for weeks at a time. Though I looked forward to letters from Paul and Fulvia, they always awoke in me that part of my heart that caused me to suffer most. I had mixed feelings when I opened a letter from Crispus, hoping that any news of my mother would be good.

> *As you know, I am in Ostia, along with Crispinianus, though not in the same century as Paul. Yesterday I sacrificed to the gods for you. Paul is gaining the esteem of his Commander as we all expected. He often speaks of you, and assures all of us that he will obtain your return among us.*
>
> *I went to see your sister and she is well. By now you must know that she has given birth to twins. Fulvia told me to reassure you that your mother is frail, but is not grave, and you should not be distressed. When I saw your mother, John, she was in bed, and was very thin and pale.*
>
> *Many have left our legion due to the command of Terentianus.*
>
> *I want to assure you that you are not alone, and that none of us will rest until you are in Rome.*
>
> *Crispus*

His letter both consoled and grieved my heart. I was comforted because those whom I loved continued to hold me in their hearts. But I was grieved, for I had not known that Fulvia had given birth, and the continued vague news of my mother's health troubled me.

\*\*\*

More months passed. I had not heard from Merytre, and this pained me, for I had grown in esteem and affection for her.

Fulvia began to write again, telling me of her family, of Paul, and of events in Rome. My sister's letters were always unclear concerning my mother; on the one hand she was ill, on the other she was well. When I inquired of Paul, he responded.

> *Your sister has told me that your mother is not well, but is not grave either. She has instructed me not to distress you. Since I am not a physician, I cannot tell you if this is the case. I believe Fulvia is doing her best to console your mother and to protect you, John. I wish I had more precise news about your mother, but this is all I know.*
>
> *Paul*

About a week after hearing from Paul, I received an urgent communication from Fulvia, in which she begged me to come to Rome immediately because my mother's illness had taken a turn, and there was fear that she would not survive the cold months. She wrote so few words, but they carried such a great weight. My life was thrown into turmoil by this news. I threw the letter down and went outside. I needed to get to Rome to be with my mother, if even for a short while. I fetched the letter again and went to my Commander to show him the communication.

"No one can be released from his duty! I was warned about you and I will not grant you any favors. Terentianus issued orders that you be treated as a new recruit, and as such you may not leave your station for any reason whatever!" As I opened my mouth to explain further, he dismissed me and called several soldiers to escort me out.

I returned to my tent. The helmet of a *tiro* was on the ground, and I kicked it so hard that I smashed the side of it. I cried aloud, "Will the curse of Terentianus follow me for my entire life?" I wondered what my course of action should be. I was so angry I could kill; I wanted to do away with any who had stood in my path. I wanted to seek out Terentianus and make him suffer and pay for what he had done to me. I dashed out of the garrison; it was well that no one spoke to me at that moment, such was my fury.

After several hours, my practice of the virtues enabled me to pause and reflect on where that path of violence would lead. In order to gain control over myself, I went to the darkness of the Mithraeum. There I sought the guidance of the god and the strength to master myself. As the hours passed inside that dark cave, two things became clear: above all else I desired to go to Rome to be with my mother, but I would not disobey my orders. I would do my duty, for only that was a sure road.

I recalled the words of Crispus in his letter concerning the fact that Paul had gained the respect of his Commander. Why was that not the case with me? It slowly dawned on me, in that darkness, that I had been remiss here in Alexandria. I was a skilled soldier and was much respected wherever I had served. I had always done what was asked of me, and far more. But here I kept mostly to myself. With no opportunity for battle, it was difficult to show one's skills; after all, I was merely guarding grain at the port, something that an animal could do.

I returned to my quarters and thought about what I had done in the past that I had neglected here. In Germania, I often practiced both my battle tactics and strategies with other soldiers, especially with the *tirones*. This had helped me to grow in skill, and them to learn new techniques, and to think more quickly in battle. In Alexandria, I practiced my skills alone. I began to realize that I had neglected my involvement with the others and had not shared any of the experience that I had gained in the legion. I had sealed myself off out of anger and frustration. This prevented me from seeing anyone or anything around me. I had not looked at the situation of our century to discover how I might improve our ability, as I had done in Germania. I reflected, then I understood that what was most lacking among my men was experience. Combat preparation was necessary, and

I would offer training to any who wished to step forward. In this way I could both better my century, and perhaps gain the esteem of my Commander.

I began to speak first to the men I shared my duties with and found there was great interest in participating in training at the end of each day. I encouraged them to tell their friends. About thirty men showed up that first afternoon. I began by asking them what they already knew of combat. I was surprised. They were ignorant of how to handle a sword and how to keep formation in battle. They knew nothing of fighting, or of thinking ahead of the enemy. In Germania, we were all eager to improve our skills, because the enemy was so close and there were many experienced soldiers. Here the men were so new that they had never seen combat. I explained to them that what I could teach them would not only make them better fighters, but could save their lives. About twenty began to come every day, and I became their unofficial instructor.

The younger recruits were eager to hear of the combat I had participated in, and the fighting strategies used in our victories. Because the Empire was now unstable, with varying power centers that were shifting, it was easy to imagine that these men would indeed see battle. I instructed them and practiced with them the handling of the various instruments of war. They were not skilled at using the *gladius*[23], which would surely doom them in a struggle with a more experienced enemy. I also sparred with them using the *spatha*[24], and threw the javelin every afternoon. These exercises benefited both them and me, for it helped me to polish my skills and to think about my experience in the field.

I had planned on training these men for sixty days, after which I would demonstrate their newly acquired skills to our

---

[23] The *gladius* was a short sword (about 60 centimeters long) used by Roman legionnaires for stabbing and slashing the enemy.
[24] The *spatha* was a longer sword (75-100 centimeters long), worn on the left side, and was used to keep the enemy at a distance. It became very popular among Roman legionnaires.

Commander, who would have no recourse but to be pleased. I hoped that I could be granted my request to take leave to Rome to care for my mother for a few months.

Enthusiasm spread. When I arrived at the place of training, I often found men already gathered, waiting with anticipation for our session to begin. Several other soldiers began to participate until our number nearly doubled. I taught the men to spar with one another, to care for their weapons, and to outsmart their enemy.

One afternoon our Commander appeared unannounced in order to watch what his men were up to after hours. He observed for some time, then left without a word. He continued to appear several times a week to see our training. He seemed content. After the fourth time, he approached me and thanked me for my work. I was pleased that I was both helping my men, and perhaps helping my cause.

Then one day a letter from Paul arrived regarding my mother.

*My brother,*

*I am well, but your mother is not. Fulvia has finally told me the whole truth. Your mother may not recover at all, but the physician is still unsure. I have offered my help to your sister. I have also been speaking with my Commander about you and am making some progress. I hope that you will be in Rome soon. You asked me to tell you all, so I am. Your mother is very ill, John. I am distressed at this, for I have been with her these past few days. I am also distressed because I know how this news will make you suffer. I want to be of assistance to you; please tell me how. Remember, in this, as in all things, you are not alone. I am with you. Crispus and Crispinianus are here now, and they salute you.*

*Paul*

Though I was consoled by the companionship of Paul, my distress grew at the news of my mother. I did not feel it was time to make a second request of my Commander. I planned an exhibition in three weeks; it was then that I would ask him again to take leave. I hoped my mother would not worsen before then. This is the plan I followed until I received an urgent communication from Fulvia.

*Dearest brother,*

*I have the saddest news to bring you. Our dear mother has died. She asked for you repeatedly, but she understood your situation and told me to reassure you not to be troubled, that you have been a good son. She has been proud of you in this life, so will she be in the next. Paul has been here visiting and consoling both me and the children. He suffers much because he is unable to be there with you to aid you in your distress. I saw him weeping in the garden this evening. We long for you to be among us, but know that the gods have deemed otherwise, for now. My husband greets you. I embrace you.*

*Fulvia*

After I read these words I went to the god I worshiped and implored him to watch over my mother in the next life, and to help me to feel nothing in this life. I stayed in that dark cave for a long time, not wanting to continue on the outside. I remembered the courage of the god, and having learned to conquer myself in these past years, I rose and returned to my duties. I resolved that I would behave as if nothing had taken place, and continue with honor in the face of adversity.

I did not respond to the communications of either my sister or Paul. Just several days later, I received another communication from Paul, which was full of sorrow and affection. I knew not how to respond because I felt like a shell, and not a man any longer. Though I felt bound to Paul, and to my sister and mother, I felt no love, nor hate, nor sorrow, nor joy. Perhaps Terentianus had won.

Months passed. I still had not heard from Merytre, and I had not responded to Paul or my sister. I felt that I was existing half way between life and death, though on the outside no one would have guessed. I continued my training as others joined in to participate. My men were becoming skilled fighters and could take on any challenge. The exhibition was held as scheduled, and I and my men were acclaimed throughout the legion for our initiative and skill. Even the Commander commended and embraced me before all the men. But it was too late to use this to my advantage.

Whenever I could get away, I fled to the Mithraeum. Perhaps it became a place to hide. Sitting there in the dark, I would resolve to seek to master myself even more, so that I could continue with my duties and not think of or desire anything. Perhaps I had found a way to move forward with part of me now dead.

I remained in this state for some time, until one day my Commander sent word for me to report at once. "John," he began, as we stood in the glaring Egyptian sun outside his quarters. "You know that I have come to value and esteem you as one of the best legionnaires in my century. You have gone beyond what has been asked, which is a rare quality for those in the provinces. I regret the reports that arrived which tarnished your reputation, and I value your role here in Alexandria. Hence it is with sorrow for me, but gladness for you, that I issue your new orders. You are to report at once to Rome to join the garrison stationed in the city itself, to take up whatever duties will be assigned. As soon as the next transport ship leaves, you are to be on it." With these words he embraced my arm and saluted me.

I found myself walking away stunned at the news, and I kept

walking until I was clear of the city and surrounded by the desolate sands. I sat and began to weep. It seemed that all the sorrow and pain that had filled my life in the past years came gushing out of my heart, and I could not stop. I do not know for how many hours I wept, but when I made my way back to my quarters, it was dusk. A large group of the men that I had trained were waiting for me. Somehow they had received word of my transfer, and they had prepared a soldier's feast of roasted meat, bread, and wine. "Behold, our leader!" one of them cried out as I approached and was embraced by each of them. I had never known affection or camaraderie in the land of the Pharaohs, yet here it was before me. Perhaps it had always been there. I was indeed surprised to see my men visibly saddened by my departure, and regretted being blind to that friendship before now. We spent the evening there, with food and song, as we celebrated my leaving this land.

I went to honor Mithras the next day, and was taken off guard once more by my brethren at the Mithraeum who had prepared a similar celebration. In honoring the god, I had found the path of discipline that I sought, but not the community of brothers that was promised. I had blamed this on being in a foreign land. Yet here they were, thirty or so of those who had worshiped Mithras with me, gathered in my honor, to celebrate my presence and departure from among them. What had I given to these men that I should be so honored? I did not understand. I posed this question to the *Pater* discreetly during the feast, and he answered, "You have gained the esteem of all here, not because of something you have done, but because of the man you are, John. Perhaps the gods have permitted you to leave at the moment when you could freely choose to stay. This is how the gods treat men. Haven't you perceived this?" I was in a daze again. On my last days in the land of the Pharaohs, my eyes were being opened. Why did it take so long for me to see what I had been given?

\*\*\*

As I boarded the ship a few days later, I hoped that I once again would learn to be alive. I was half way between my past and my future, belonging to neither. How the orders for my transfer came about was a mystery to me, but I was sure that Paul had somehow made it happen. As the ship pushed off and the coast of Egypt faded into the horizon, I turned away to face the direction of Rome. When I thought of Paul and Fulvia, I felt nothing. "I should be happy that I am going to see those I love," I thought to myself. I was still burdened by the past, like an extra bundle had found itself onto the ship and into my things, and inside my heart.

During the voyage, I was expected to be responsible for a number of tasks on the ship and I fulfilled my duty as I always had. At night I would go on deck and gaze at the stars. It seemed that all the gods in the heavens were looking down on me. I wondered which one had been leading me through these past years in order that I might become stronger and master of myself. I sought to make sense of my time in the land of the Pharaohs by thinking of Mithras and my Commander and legion. There were lessons in all these.

On some evenings, I remembered Merytre and our long conversations about Egypt and the gods, as well as happiness and sorrow. I was saddened I could not bid her farewell, because I did not approach the inn again, so as not to provoke the wrath of her father. But the affection I had for her I still carried with me.

Under that starry sky, I thought of Paul. I had such gratitude and love for him; his affection and loyalty had sustained me. Though I had distanced myself even from him after the death of my mother, I knew that it was in him that my heart had a place of rest.

One evening the captain approached me, and we stood silently for a long time, gazing at the sea and the sky. "Returning to Rome for good?" he inquired.

"Not returning, because I've never been to Rome. But my family is there and I am eager to join them.

He continued, "If you're retiring from the legion, I could use a big, strong man like you on my team. I'm Flavius. I know you are John. I make it my business to know who is on my ship. Ever think of working on the sea, soldier?" I laughed, for it was among the last things I would ever want to do.

"No, Captain, I'm not leaving the legion at all. I'm being stationed in Rome." There was silence for a time as we gazed out. It was a peaceful night. I turned to him and asked, "Captain, where is your home?" He smiled and paused for a long time. He was shorter than I and stoutly built, with an unkempt black beard and long hair.

"This is home, John. Right on this ship. When I started sailing twenty some years ago, I would have said that Brindisi was my home, for that is where I started out, and I spent my childhood near the port. But the past few years, I've grown accustomed to Alexandria. Such a beautiful, clean, white city. Some say it is more beautiful than Rome. When you see Rome, John, you might just long to be back in Alexandria." I laughed. He continued, "Where I spend most of my time, and where I enjoy being the most, is right here. So this is home, between two worlds, but belonging to none.

There was another pause and I replied, "Well, that's exactly how I feel."

He turned to me and asked, "Who do you have waiting for you in Rome, John? Wife? Children? Brothers?

"I have a sister and … a brother," was my reply. "And I have not seen them in three years. My mother died while I was stationed in Egypt…" I trailed off. We both continued to gaze out silently. It was a time not for speech, but only for looking out at the stars.

# Chapter 3: Return

A few days later, the Captain approached me and said, "We should see the coast of Italy tomorrow, and we will land either tomorrow or the next day. I've sent word ahead so that preparations can be made to unload the ship. Sure you won't consider my offer, John?" I thanked him, but it was out of the question.

I anxiously waited to sight land, and the coast came into view toward the end of the next day, which meant we would land the following morning. Because the grain we carried was to be brought to Ostia, I had no clear plan of how I would get to Rome, or how I would contact Paul and Fulvia once I was there, because I did not know the city. But I was sure that they would find me.

It was a cloudless, warm day as preparations were made to land. A few other passengers and I were loaded onto several smaller boats and rowed toward the port. The unloading of the grain was a longer process, so the passengers were dispensed with first. As we approached, there seemed to be much movement and shouting as the port workers prepared for the grain shipment. When we landed, we were largely unnoticed. I gathered up my things and turned to make my way toward the town when I looked up and saw, fifty paces in front of me, Paul, Fulvia, Crispus, and Crispinianus. Fulvia ran toward me while the others froze, as we looked at one another in disbelief. My sister reached me first, then all approached and embraced me with great emotion. I stood back and looked at them; all were weeping, Paul included! I began to make a joke and said, "I thought my return would bring you joy, not sorrow!" and when I said this, first Fulvia, then the others, stopped. They looked at me, then at one another, all with wet eyes, and began to laugh. We stood there a while and continued to look at one another, scarcely believing that we were together once more. Crispus and Crispinianus had grown to look even more like brothers. Fulvia was beautiful as always, but she had lines of worry on her face, and this caused me sorrow. Paul was the powerful man he had always been, taller than all of us, with a soldier's bearing that made those he approached move to one side. All of a sudden, the four of them picked me up, although Fulvia did not help very much, and carried me toward the town, where my sister had arranged our transportation to Rome. It was good to be with those who were like a family to me.

\*\*\*

On the road to Rome, it seemed that all were speaking at once; such was the joy of seeing one another. My own heart seemed to thaw, as I looked around at the faces of those who held me in their hearts. Crispus still laughed much; Crispinianus was quiet as always. Paul and Fulvia were bubbling over, and I sat there amongst them, content, and at peace.

Paul came to sit next to me and put his arm around my shoulder. As he turned towards me to speak, looking me in the eyes, he began to weep once again. His tears echoed my own. After a time we spoke words to one another which remain locked in my heart.

We had left Ostia and were approaching Rome. As I looked about, I was disappointed, for I expected large buildings covered with marble, with gardens and wide streets. Instead, we passed one lodging built upon another, without any order at all. There was much noise, piles of garbage, and terrible odors. Paul, knowing my thoughts, turned and said, "Wait brother. The Rome of the Caesars lies beyond." We continued through the rough, narrow streets, dodging animals and beggars, children and refuse.

After a while, Paul said, "Let us get out here and walk," and we all descended from our wagon onto a small street. We proceeded and, turning a corner, found ourselves in that main place called the Forum.

\*\*\*

The smells and litter of the surrounding areas gave way to clean streets and buildings that rivaled those in Alexandria. In fact, the city in Egypt seemed to be a smaller version of Rome. As we walked down the main road, I found myself always looking up, for the edifices were so tall that they drew one's eyes to the heavens. Paul put his hand on my shoulder to guide me as I moved forward, gazing at Rome's wonders. It was like a dream.

We passed great temples and public buildings, shops and stalls, buyers and sellers, and even more tongues spoken in one place than in Alexandria. The diversity of peoples, both citizens and slaves, was most impressive.

Like Alexandria, it was said that some parts of the city were falling into neglect, but there was no sign of that here. Paul told us that Constantine himself had initiated a number of building projects which were apparent as we made our way.

Paul had grown more mature than when I had seen him last. He was entering into the fullness of his manhood, yet his easy laugh and passion for life remained. "John, come, let me show you more wonders," he said, as he led me toward the palace of the Emperor, the ancient dwelling of the vestals, and the stadium of Flavius. He and Fulvia laughed as my mouth hung open. I wondered how man could have created such things.

At this point, Fulvia turned and kissed me, and said, "I must take leave of you, beloved brother. Welcome to your home." Indeed, she now had children who, along with her husband of the patrician class, consumed much of her time and energy. We all bade her farewell as Paul and I headed for our garrison, and Crispus and Crispinianus toward theirs. We agreed to meet later that evening.

\*\*\*

We would be stationed near the center of the city, and as we approached that place we encountered many soldiers who, to my surprise, did not look Roman at all. "The Empire is changing," Paul said, "but fear not. These may look more like barbarians than Romans, but their hearts are with the Empire, and you can trust them. You will see."

Paul introduced me to the others in our garrison, as well as to my new Commander. They all showed great respect to Paul, and esteem for me. It was as if my new garrison also had been awaiting my arrival with anticipation.

My Commander granted me some time of rest before taking up my new duties.

Over the next few days, Paul and I spoke of our time apart, he in Gaul, then Rome, and I in Egypt. The letters we had written could not capture the experiences that had taken hold of us. I told him of the Mythraeum, of my wondering about the meaning of these events, of Merytre, of my reaction to the death of my mother. He also told me of the obstacles he had to face, feeling in exile in Gaul. He too had to break out of the mold that Terentianus had cast him in. He revealed to me the anxiety that he suffered for me, and his growing determination to change that situation. It was good to be with Paul; the understanding we had of each other was a rare gift.

\*\*\*

A few days after my arrival, Fulvia asked me to visit her. "I would like to accompany you," Paul stated, and so we went together. I had not been to her home yet, had not met her husband or children, and had not been in the room where our mother had spent the last days of her life. Paul had always been extremely protective of me and I assumed that he wanted to come to shield me from sorrow.

Fulvia's was a nice home by Roman standards, with a courtyard filled with fragrant plants and flowers which she loved. "John," she cried, as she ran and embraced me. "This is my husband, Gaius Byzantius," she said, as a patrician-looking man in his forties stepped forward to greet me. Two children then ran out and right up to Paul, pulling him down, and immediately sitting on his lap. Paul was such a large man, and the children so small, that the sight was comical. He seemed a Hercules with two Cupids.

"You are always welcome here, John. As you can see, Paul has already become part of our family!" Gaius said. I sat down so as not to intimidate the children, and Fulvia introduced me to them. Nonetheless, they were afraid of me, probably because I had a soldier's bearing, and they did not understand my relationship with their mother. It saddened me that I had not been a part of their lives from the beginning, but I was determined to make up for lost time. I presented them with some small gifts from Egypt; they ran off to examine them in some secret place where children are apt to flee. Fulvia then asked us to quietly follow her to a shady corner of the garden, where her recently born twins were sleeping soundly. We gazed at them, then crept back to the fountain and sat.

Gaius excused himself because he had to attend to some business at his ministry, but extracted a promise to return for dinner the following evening. He seemed a kind and considerate man, but very rushed that first time we met. Fulvia, Paul, and I sat in the garden as the sun warmed the carved stones and butterflies sought out the sweetness of Fulvia's flowers. We relished the beauty of the garden and the warmth of one another's companionship.

"Fulvia," I said after some time, "I wish to see her room." I had not mourned my mother's death because I had built a wall around my heart. But in this house the reality of my mother's life and death were more present; I needed to see her room; I needed to feel her presence one more time.

Paul sat next to me and said, "Little brother, both of us only want joy for you in Rome after so much sorrow away. I want to spare you this; *we* want to spare you this." I realized Paul's concern, for he knew my heart like no other.

"I wish you could," I replied as I stood up and made my way toward that room.

Fulvia had kept my mother's things in place: her mirror, for she always took a look at herself before leaving home, even if it was to step out the door for a moment. Her comb, in which a few of her hairs were still caught, was there. I lifted it, and could smell her odor. I held onto it as I sat on her bed and took up her favorite tunic, which was lying on a chair. Her sweet, motherly scent was also still caught up in the fabric. As I smelled it, I wept, and then sobbed. My fortress was breaking down. Paul sat next to me to comfort me, and Fulvia knelt before me. As I calmed, Paul nodded to Fulvia, who left the room and returned with a small box.

\*\*\*

"Before she died, mamma told me to give this to you. She said it should remind you how proud she was, and how much she loved you. She said it would make you less sorrowful, for it would remind you that she is now with those who love her." She handed the box to me.

I was astonished as I opened it. "Papa's ring!" I exclaimed. I had few memories of my father, because he had died when I was so young. But my mother had often spoken of him, as he was the one who had conquered her heart. It was the ring that he wore for her, which she had often shown to us as children. It was her most-prized possession, her connection with her love that had passed beyond. As I took the ring into my hand, I wept again. If I had forgotten how to feel in Egypt, here I was feeling too much.

I walked slowly with Paul back to our garrison. I knew not what to say, nor did he, but our companionship was enough. Arriving back at my quarters, I put the ring in a safe place and went about my duties.

Paul had arranged a position for me as trainer of the new recruits in Rome. The next day, I was determined to begin to prepare. I wanted to get to know the men I was going to instruct, but still had some time before the actual training began. Each man confronted battle in a different way, and I wanted to discover this within the men I would be responsible for. Even Paul and I were different in these matters. Anger fueled me in fighting the enemy; my rage became the energy which would keep me strong and on my feet for days, if necessary. For Paul, battle was something of an adventure, something that he reveled in, like a sport. We were both effective soldiers, but confronted the task differently.

As I was making my rounds of the men, some days after my visit to my sister, I returned to my quarters around sunset and found my things out of place. I was alarmed to find that my father's ring had been stolen. I ran out and inquired of those around whether they had seen anyone enter. They described a stranger in the garrison who was dressed in the attire of a soldier. They did not question him, assuming he was a visitor. "He just left a short time ago, in that direction," one told me. I grabbed my sword and my dagger and ran at full strength until I sighted a man hurrying toward the center of the city. I was convinced he was the thief because he wore a soldier's cloak, but no other military attire. Determined to get the ring back at any cost, I circled around him, hiding behind the buildings, and even going down another street, keeping pace with him. He did not notice me. When I surpassed him, I doubled back, put my hand on my sword, turned the corner, and stepped in front of him. As he attempted to flee to the side, I flipped my sword and put the tip under his chin. He stood still in fear. I pushed it in until his blood spurted out on his chest, but not enough to seriously injure him.

"I have nothing! Help!" he began to shout. With my other hand, I whipped out my dagger and slashed his wrist deeply; his clenched fist let go of the ring.

"I should kill you now," I said as I stepped closer, twisting my sword, moving the tip deeper into his flesh. More blood gushed out as he cried out once again. He did not have the courage of a soldier, so I surmised that he had also stolen the garb he wore in order to enter the garrison unnoticed. As I looked at him, frightened and pleading, I thought to myself, "Who would know? Aren't I justified in taking his life?" I was so angry I almost plunged my sword all the way in at that moment. Then I stopped and mastered my anger. I stood back, but held my sword fast under his chin. "If I ever see you again, I will kill you," I told him. I sent him off, clutching his throat and coughing, dripping with his own blood.

Paul had heard of the incident and met me on my way back. I was still breathing hard and was upset by the whole occurrence, but Paul was furious.

"What did he do to you? Where is he? Did he injure you?" he asked me, his fury building. I looked down to see my arm covered with blood.

"I am fine, Paul. This is his blood, not mine. The matter is finished," I said. But Paul was just getting started. He had his sword drawn, and was insistent on setting out and finding the thief, and killing the man himself.

"I can just follow his blood. Look, it leads toward the

western part of the city. What a fool! Is he a soldier? I could easily track him down then..." Paul was fuming because he was protective of me, but he also enjoyed a fight. I had to restrain him from pursuing the matter. Just as my anger could get me into trouble, Paul's passion could lead him too far. We were not on the battlefield here. We were in Rome and different rules prevailed.

"I need you to accompany me to Fulvia's home," I said to him, in order to distance ourselves from the matter. He consented, so we made our way to my sister's so I could turn the ring over to her for safekeeping.

\*\*\*

As the days passed, I took up my new duties with the soldiers entrusted to me. It was a task I had already done well in the past, so I began with much confidence in the ability of the new soldiers to learn. Some of them were experienced, but had not seen combat in years. Others were new recruits with enthusiasm, but no skills. I endeavored to forge bonds with them and encouraged the men to do so with one another, for this was the strength of the legion.

My training program was simple. On some days, I would teach them of the battles of the past and the tactics used. I would then present situations on the battlefield that they would someday confront, and we would apply the knowledge learned from battles of history to outwit the enemy in the present. On other days, I trained them about various weapons, on how to keep in physical condition while awaiting orders, and many other matters concerning a soldier's state.

Most of the day was spent on the physical practice in which they would spar with one another and with me, using every conceivable weapon, even sticks, in case they ever lost their *gladius*. I worked them hard, but not to excess, and every month we put on an exhibition at which they could show their skills to the other men, as well as to their friends throughout the city. I was enjoying myself, and so were the men.

A few weeks later, I had the occasion to ask Paul how he had obtained my release from Egypt. "I was not successful in becoming a commander," he began, as we sat in a quiet Roman street under the summer stars, "because I soon realized that being a skillful soldier has nothing to do with such an appointment. It became clear to me how Terentianus rose in the ranks so quickly, despite the fact that he had seen so little battle, and had no care for his men at all. It is the politics of Rome, my brother. These appointments are not given to those with greater ability, but rather depend on one's family line, or the influential friends one has made along the way. I did not realize that this permeated the military when I first arrived here. On the very first day, I marched into my Commander's office and demanded that the injustice inflicted upon you by Terentianus be undone, and that you be sent to Rome at once. He looked at me oddly and said he would look into the matter. As time passed and nothing changed, I learned that these commanders rarely disagree with one another. It is as if, realizing that others would serve as more effective commanders, they shield one another from criticism. I am certain, in fact, that my Commander and Terentianus were friends. My heart then fell; it was as if part of me were in Egypt suffering with you, and the other part were here, angry over my inability to effect any change. I felt helpless, so I sought out your sister."

At this point, we rose and began to walk as Paul continued. "Fulvia suggested that the road to obtain your release would be longer than we anticipated, so we decided to combine our efforts to bring it about. I would work hard in order to gain respect, so that my words and opinions would carry some weight. I thought that I could find a way to make the Commander simply order your return. Fulvia resolved to pressure her husband to use his influence around the city. This is how we set out to get you here, John. You understand, do you not, that I was willing to do anything to obtain your coming to Rome, not only to ease your suffering, but my own?" At this point, Paul looked down and we paused before a temple, white columns gleaming in the night. We were both aware that our lives were linked in an extraordinary way. We then continued down the street.

Paul chuckled. "I soon realized that it would be impossible for me to obtain the post of commander, due to my 'humble birth,' and the fact that all my friends were soldiers. I was also told one day that my attitude would prevent me from gaining any important position, right after I had blurted out among my men, 'I haven't a drop of patrician blood running through these veins! My ancestors kept as far from patricians as men do vipers. I am proud to say that patrician blood has never soiled my family line!' Yes, I was joking, but there was a grain of truth nonetheless. Those who put on airs, or are favored simply due to an accident of birth, rather than any brave deeds, are to be laughed at, not honored. And you know me, brother. When I have an opinion, it is difficult for me to keep it to myself. So it became known that I did not revere the patrician class as others are wont to do when they seek political appointments. I cannot help being myself, John. So I had to find another way."

We approached the Tiber and walked along its banks. Paul continued, "I began doing again what I do best: being a soldier. It was only in this way that I gained the esteem of my men and eventually the respect of my Commander. It was known that I was always open to a new escapade, and so I would often volunteer for those tasks which took me away from my normal duties. Even if it simply meant accompanying an official outside of the city, I would volunteer. Firstly, because of you, and secondly, well, you know how I love an adventure. Even the possibility of battling brigands was exciting to me. Most of the time, I saw no fighting at all. But my willingness to take on tasks that the other men shunned gained me the eye of the Commander. I eventually earned his trust, to the point that he began to ask my opinion on various military appointments, which I willingly gave, as you can imagine! Once I had his ear it was just a matter of time before I began speaking with him about the need for greater training of the men, especially those stationed in and around Rome, who would be lost if they were ever sent to fight, because they either had no experience at all or were growing soft. Once I convinced him of this, I told him I would take the responsibility of setting up the training, and that I knew the one man who would be effective in this task, and that man is you. Telling you this now seems so simple. It is not even clear to me why it took three years to bring about. But that is what happened. So I am not a commander. I do not want to be a commander. I am happy here, and am happy that you are here."

We turned and began walking uphill as Paul continued. "I came to see Fulvia as a sister. When I went to her home, we found ourselves always speaking of you. It seemed that you were present, even if only in our memories. When her children were born, I was among the first to visit her. Her husband, though a patrician, is a kind man. He would laugh at us sometimes as she and I would sit scheming for hours on how to steal you from Egypt. Three years of scheming." Paul laughed. Then he turned and looked at me. "I was there when your mother was ill, John. I went to the house whenever I had some free moments from my duties. I wanted to be strong for them and for you, though you were far away. I do not want to relive those moments, but I will tell you this: your mother died in peace. She was not in anguish or sad. In fact, she seemed grateful for her life. Even though you were in Egypt, she spoke of you as if you were in the next room. She was so proud of you. I know, John, that her love will always be with you." At this he smiled, and we both reflected on his words and our memories. Then he looked at me. "So that is the past, this is the present. Let us rejoice in the present," and we turned to walk back to the soldiers' quarters.

\*\*\*

The life of Rome is in the streets, for most Romans' dwellings were even more humble than a soldier's. After finishing our duties, we often went out to observe the various peoples, entertainment, and events which animated the city. Though many lived in squalor, the public places were worthy of an Emperor. The wide roads with marble temples and buildings, the large plazas encircled with columns and trees, the banks of the Tiber with their shops and boats, these were all lit up at night for the people of Rome. Those were evenings of friendship, for I often met Crispus and Crispinianus, and sometimes even Fulvia and her husband and children, as we partook of the excitement.

"John!" Paul called from a nearby street where he had wandered one evening. I approached with Crispus and Crispinianus (at this point nicknamed "the brothers" by their own garrison, though they continued to deny any relation) and mingled with the crowd watching the spectacle. As the Romans recognized us as soldiers, they opened up for us as a man flew high into the air, flipping over, and landed on his feet, to our astonishment. The performers seemed, due to their appearance, to be from one of the eastern provinces, and were attempting to earn the few coins the crowd might leave. They continued to perform seemingly impossible feats. I wondered if I could accomplish any of them, because I was both strong and fast on the battlefield. "Would you like to fight like that?" Paul asked, reading my thoughts. "There goes John, over the heads of the enemy!" he said jokingly, motioning with his arm. The image he invoked made all of us break into such fits of laughter that all four of us had to withdraw from the crowd, because we were distracting from the spectacle.

\*\*\*

Although gladiatorial combat had been outlawed in the

Empire,[25] many, but especially soldiers, maintained a passion for that sport, and mock battles were often held in which no one was hurt. Those shows were common among the street performers of Rome, but were often more comic than dramatic. The four of us often found ourselves watching such spectacles in the evenings. Once, Fulvia happened upon us. After greeting me and the others, she noticed the mock battle that we were watching. She looked at the show, then back at us. We all stood there smiling. Shaking her head, she turned back toward her home, saying, "Soldiers!" as she threw up her hands. I suppose it was the absence of combat that drew us to such spectacles.

The next day Paul and I went to honor Mithras at the temple near the baths. As I sat in the darkness, I realized that I had less recourse to the god than in Egypt. I had not rejected the discipline or what I had learned before, but did not much think of the need for anything else. Suffering and loneliness brought me to seek out the world of the unseen. Now in Rome, I was content, and hoped for no more than what I had been given. But I was not remiss. I thanked the god for keeping Paul and Fulvia as well as Crispus and Crispinianus safe.

As days turned into weeks and then months, my training was going well. I quickly won the esteem of my men and Commanders on my own merits. I strove to teach the soldiers to work as one, as we had in Germania. This would be our strength.

After my training was finished, I would return to the barracks where I would either find Paul, or would await his arrival. The quarters became a gathering point for many friends. We were all soldiers, and were often eager to leave the barracks to attend the races or baths, or simply to enjoy one another's companionship in the streets. There were often fifteen or more of us together, laughing and making the most of our being in the city of the Caesars. If Crispus was along, there was sure to be joking.

---

[25] Constantine outlawed gladiatorial combat throughout the Empire in 325 C.E.

"Recall how frightened you would become as I would whisper to you from outside your tent! You thought it was the gods calling you to fly!" he taunted Paul one evening. Notwithstanding the fact that Crispus had grown into a powerful man, Paul scooped him up and threw him upon his shoulders and ran down toward the Tiber until Crispus beseeched him not to throw him in! Paul let him down, and they began to sing together as we walked. Such was the camaraderie we enjoyed in those days.

I was less closed in on myself here than I had been in Alexandria. Paul tends to draw my personality out, because by nature I am quieter than he is. Perhaps this is another reason why I so quickly won the respect of others here in Rome.

"What will you do after the military John," one friend asked me one evening while we were together.

"A quiet life, perhaps on a farm," I said. I then laughed and continued, "I joined the legion to escape the farm, and now I look forward to a quiet life among my pigs and vegetables!"

"Do you come from farmer's stock?" I was asked by another.

"Yes, my father. It is in the blood," I said, and smiled.

"What about you, Paul? You come from farmer's stock also?" the others asked. Paul grew quiet and let the question pass. He was sensitive about his past, and rarely spoke of it. I knew that the death of his parents made his life difficult at a young age. The uncle who raised him instilled in him the dream of joining the legion, which he did when he was seventeen. Three years later his uncle died, and Paul was alone. The legion became his family, the soldiers his brothers. I knew these things were difficult for him.

"He comes from farmer's stock," I answered for him.

"He looks more like he could take on Hercules than a plow," another continued, and all, including Paul, laughed.

That same evening we walked through the city; there was an area in which soldiers usually gathered and took food. Paul took nothing.

"Have you no hunger or thirst?" I asked.

"No money. I will eat at the barracks later," he replied. I would not allow him to be the only one among us without food, so I provided for him.

"We received our pay only two days ago. Why are you without money?" I pressed him. He was silent. The next day I inquired further, and discovered that one of our companions was in need due to circumstances in his family. Paul, having heard this, gave all of his pay to this man.

"Why did you keep nothing for yourself?" I asked Paul later.

"Because his need was greater," was his reply. This was the character of Paul, and this was his typical way of reasoning. Though a strong and even ferocious fighter, he was also compassionate and protective of others in our garrison. He was loyal beyond all measure, and this gained him the respect and affection of all who knew him.

\*\*\*

Months had passed when I was surprised to receive a letter from Egypt; it was from Merytre. She had given it to one of the men in my garrison there who had forwarded it to me. I opened it and read:

*Dearest John,*

*It is with sadness for me, but happiness for you, that I learned of your departure. I had hoped that we would be able to see each other again, and was waiting for the opportunity to contact you. When I finally sent a message to you to meet me at the inn, I learned that you were no longer here. I wept.*

*Life here continues as always. I know things are much better for you now, because you are with those you love. For this I am glad. I will always think of you with gratitude in my heart. You have taught me many things, and I no longer look at Romans in the same way. In fact, I have come to see my life itself differently.*

*My parents have informed me that I am to marry a man I have never met, in less than a year. It is the custom here, although I was hoping to escape this tradition. But I have resigned myself to do my duty. When they informed me of this decision, I thought about our walk through Alexandria that night, and your questions to me became my questions to myself. Perhaps it is true that doing one's duty is for all, but to find happiness is only for a few.*

*Merytre*

I put the letter down, and I was sad. I did not respond to it right away because I knew not what to answer. "Maybe she is right," Paul said. "I do not want to surrender to the obstacles the gods put before us," he continued. "You have always sought to do your duty, as I have mine. If that were enough, we would have never suffered so much to bring you here, and you would not have longed so intensely to be here now. I refused to simply surrender to duty when your happiness was at stake, John. I will always fight for it, for you and with you. I am sorry for your friend. Perhaps she has no one to fight for her. You have one here who will always champion you, John, and I know I have the same in you. Could that not be what happiness is?" We let that question hang, for neither of us could answer it.

# Chapter 4: Germania Again

None of us could make much sense of the politics within the Empire, but we had heard that there was a struggle ensuing between Constantine and Licinius [26] over authority. Neither was in Rome, making this conflict seem far away from the cares of our lives, until some of our men began to be called up for duty. Since we had pledged ourselves to the Empire, we did not hesitate in our support for Constantine. When the orders came down to us, my life changed immediately. The hours I devoted to the men's training became longer, and the time we had for our own amusement shrank. The excitement and dread of war permeated the legion like a mist.

"No, not again!" Fulvia cried, when Paul and I told her that we had received orders to return to Germania in preparation for the conflict.

"This time it will not be so long. I will return soon," I reassured her, not knowing if my words had any truth to them at all.

Tears streamed down her face, and it pained me greatly to see her so sorrowful. "Take care of my brother, Paul."

I laughed and said, "I will be the one who will take care of him!" and Fulvia smiled. "I needed that smile before I left," I

---

[26] Licinius was raised to Augustus and adopted by Diocletian in 308 C.E. He struggled to maintain his rule first against Maximinus II Daia with the help of Constantine, but he later incited a revolt against Constantine, eventually leading to Costantine ordering the execution of Licinius in 325 C.E.

said, and turned as Paul and I made our way back to our men. Though I hated to cause my sister pain, I did not dread battle. It would be a welcome relief after these last years of inactivity.

When we arrived back at our quarters, the whole century was running to and fro, getting ready to pull out at sunrise. I too was excited and looked forward to real combat. My enthusiasm, however, was nothing compared to that of Paul, who was beside himself with anticipation. He was relishing the adventure.

I was concerned about how my men would be feeling, because they had never faced an enemy. I made my way to the new recruits' quarters to learn how they were faring. I found several of them slowly packing their things, which was not a good sign. I sensed their fear and nervousness. "Commander," one called to me. I was not officially their commander, but that is what they called me. "Will you be with us in Germania?" he asked. Several others gathered around at this question, with anxious expressions.

"Yes, I will make sure that we are together during the fighting. Do not fear; if you carry fear with you, your enemy will sense it and will triumph. Know that you are stronger than the one you face. I have taught you how to do battle and how to work together; I will not abandon you, but you must not abandon one another. You have all the skills that you need in order to overcome the enemy. Now it is up to you; the rest is in your head," I said as I tapped the forehead of the nearest soldier. "Courage is a decision, my men," I continued. "It is not how you feel, but what you decide. Many times I have faced the enemy with a fluttering heart, but I still pushed forward with ferocity. Do not forget that courage is a decision." After this, I asked to inspect their weapons to be sure all was ready. It was, so I took my leave.

At dawn we departed, marching north toward the ensuing conflict. I stopped and gazed at Rome before we completely lost sight of her. "The days of joy were so short," I said to Paul, next to me. "I wonder if the words of Merytre were a prophecy…" We both stood in silence, wondering what turns our lives would take this time.

"One thing is certain. If you are sent to Egypt once again, I am coming with you!" Paul said. We turned to rejoin my men. They would need words of encouragement along the way.

\*\*\*

Our orders reached us; our task would be to stabilize the borders of the Empire in the north, because the age-old problem of the barbarian invasions continued. The barbarians were causing havoc in the region, and the Emperor wanted to secure the area before turning east. This seemed wise.

Paul and I were seasoned in this type of battle. I encouraged my men with this news, because fighting a known enemy was always simpler than fighting an unknown one. Paul was a bit disappointed; he wanted a new adversary. "I am certain we will encounter the forces from the east soon enough," I told him. He patted me between the shoulders, as was his custom, and we marched on.

\*\*\*

As we approached our destination, we became aware of the movement of many soldiers, several legions in fact, as Constantine prepared for a two part battle: the Barbarians in the north, and the troops of Licinius in the east. We learned more about the disagreement between Constantine and Licinius; the latter was angry that Constantine sent his troops to pursue the Goths into Thrace. Licinius regarded this as his territory, and objected to the actions of Constantine, forming a conspiracy against the latter.[27] In this way the battles began.

Our century was the first to arrive at the encampment, and

---

[27] Eusebius, *Vita Constantinae*. 50. The account of Eusebius focuses more on the supposed treachery of Licinius, rather than on Constantine's move to consolidate the Empire.

also the first to hear much bitter news. A commander and a small band of men had been given the task to meet and accompany Constantina, daughter of the Emperor, to *Augusta Treverorum*, where her father was awaiting her. She was to cross into Germania in secret, because most *centuriae* had not yet arrived from the south, and her safety could not be assured, should she make a public journey. The plan was that she would travel quickly and lightly, so as to arrive before anyone knew that she had left. But apparently the news had preceded her, for Licinius was aware of her journey, and had formed a plan of his own.

Constantina and her escort had been journeying for several days. At a certain point, we know not how, they found themselves surrounded by a group of soldiers under the banner of Licinius. A battle ensued, and most of the soldiers assigned to guard the Emperor's daughter were killed, with one escaping. The news he carried was that Constantina had been taken hostage, and Licinius intended to bargain with Constantine for her release.

News of these terrible events had reached our camp within a day of their occurrence. "Were they the old Praetorian? Have they no brains at all? How could they proceed without patrolling the road ahead?" Paul burst out. We in the legion hated the Praetorian because they had been bodies without minds, strength without strategy. When something went wrong on the battlefield, we often said that it was the Praetorian influence which had caused it. Constantine, knowing these things, had abolished the Praetorian Guard after his victory near Rome. But these men who lost Constantina were not Praetorian; they were our own, which made this event more shameful.

***

It would take days, perhaps even a week, for reinforcements to arrive to mount an all out assault, but the life of the Emperor's daughter was in danger, and she would be far from our grasp by then. It was night. Paul approached and asked to speak in seclusion, outside our camp. He began, "John, we have been in perilous situations before and have survived; we have always completed successfully any mission entrusted to us. What happened to Constantina is dishonorable." He paused and looked at me. I could see, even in the darkness, that his mind was racing. He continued, "Let us, you and I, seek her out and bring her to her father. Perhaps in secret we can be more effective than an entire cohort. We know this territory better than anyone else. We could find the trail of those who have taken her, and overtake them before they reach the protection of Licinius. If we are not successful, our Commander will mount an all out assault. If we succeed, then Constantina will be safe, and we will have hope of victory. If we do this, we must act at once. What do you think?" Of course I accepted readily, and we convinced our Commander to agree to our plan. In the meantime, he would wait for the reinforcements to arrive. If we succeeded, it would be a way for him to glorify himself. He would claim that it was his initiative, but this did not matter to us. We were determined to find Constantina. Hence we gathered our supplies and horses and set out in search of the enemy.

*** 

The fact that Constantina was taken in order to force the hand of her father to grant concessions to Licinius aided us in our search, for we knew where the camp of Licinius lay, and hence the direction in which his soldiers would be heading. Our urgency was to reach her before they reached their destination, so we rode at full speed all night.

We knew there were at least twelve soldiers guarding her, and only two of us. We also knew that sentries would be posted, so that, when we approached the area we suspected they would be in, we would need to proceed with stealth, even on foot.

Before dawn broke, we stopped in order to grant some rest

both to us and our horses. Although we knew the general direction in which the party must have traveled, we did not know precisely which path they had taken. Daylight was necessary before we proceeded.

Because we were outnumbered, we would need to find a way to overcome them while avoiding fighting all twelve at once. If we could surprise them, we would have the advantage, because the enemy would not expect such a speedy pursuit with so few men.

\*\*\*

As soon as there was some hint of light, we sought signs of the passing of the marauders. I had learned tracking skills in the legion, and after searching the area for a time, I found the signs of horses. We were now on the trail of our enemy, and made quicker progress, moving forward while keeping watch that we were not spotted by sentries.

When it was past midday, we dismounted and secured our horses, for Paul had a sense that our enemies were close. We kept ourselves concealed on high ground, and listened attentively for any indication of a human presence. We crept through the trees and brush for hours, until, at a certain point, we heard distant voices. We proceeded carefully and listened for a long time in order to discern whether it was the enemy. As we stole forward, we heard loud speech and laughter. We continued to listen and caught words that indicated these were of Licinius. We became more certain that we had found our group when we heard the voice of a woman. Paul nodded. We found the enemy and the daughter of Constantine. We were thankful that their tone indicated that it did not even occur to them that they had been followed.

In battle, patience is as important as fury, so we decided to wait until night, following them at a distance until they set up their camp. They seemed to be an undisciplined group of soldiers, and that would work to our advantage.

We assessed the situation as the sun descended. There were no settlements nearby and few journeyed here. We realized that we had two advantages: the carelessness of the soldiers, and our familiarity with this territory. As the night approached, the sounds of nature rose. We would wait until that part of the night when even the animals grew quiet, and then we would approach their camp so that we could decide the most effective means to remove Constantina with minimum commotion.

Night fell and we waited. It was cloud-covered and dark, and we would turn this to our advantage. We waited and waited, not speaking a word. After some hours, Paul nodded to me and we struck out.

It seemed it took us hours to approach the enemy camp, as we proceeded so slowly and carefully. There were the remnants of a fire in whose light I could see two tents, and six soldiers sleeping outside. We crept further, encircling the camp, until we spotted the place where one sentry was posted. These were indeed careless soldiers. It was essential that we kept our advantage by surprising them in our attack. Keeping their horses quiet would be a great challenge.

We withdrew to formulate our plan. "John, you can calm a horse like no other. Can you secure their horses and, when you hear my signal, take them all to our meeting point? Thus we do not have to slay them all, just disable them from pursuing us. I will find Constantina in one of the tents and will kill those guarding her. We will both ride out and meet you. Just don't forget to leave me a horse!" he said, smiling. We agreed to this, though I hesitated because Paul was putting himself in great danger. But there was no time to discuss this concern, for the task was greater than my worries. If all went according to plan, we would then ride north, so as to trick our enemy into thinking we were moving toward *Augusta Treverorum*. They would then alert their Commander, and their forces would follow. After one day, we would turn south to bring Constantina safely into Rome.

Because I had been raised on a farm, I was able to approach the enemy's horses and win their trust with minimal noise or movement. I had to first be calm myself in order to do this, for they would sense any fear. I found fourteen steeds and two sleeping soldiers, at a distance, that we had not accounted for. I suppressed my anxiety, and stood with the animals as I waited for Paul's signal. When that came, I would ride at full speed and bring all the horses to the rendezvous point. I would then scatter them in different directions.

As I waited, the passing of time was agonizing. There were at least twelve men in the camp. Against them all was Paul, creeping into their encampment. Because they were unaware of being followed, perhaps they were as careless as the soldiers who had lost Constantina. At least, I hoped so. As the time passed, I went through the steps of our escape one by one, and prayed to the gods to watch over this deed. As the night grew deeper, and I more nervous, I heard a yell, and then voices, and a cry. I heard Paul shout, not out of fear, but his yell of triumph as he tried to terrorize the enemy with his voice before he did so with his sword. Before the two sleeping soldiers were on their feet, I jumped on a horse, and dragged the others behind me, as we galloped to the other side of the hill and into the adjoining valley. Behind me, I heard screams and the clashing of swords. Gods, help us now!

I arrived in the valley and waited. I could no longer hear any sounds, only the deep silence of death, which made me shudder. I renewed my devotion to the gods. "If you help us succeed, o powerful gods who hold us in your hands, I vow that my life will not be in vain! I will honor you with my life and my death; this I promise," I prayed, without then knowing the implications of what I was saying. The minutes seemed like hours as I waited, attentive to any sound, any indication of the outcome. How long should I wait, I wondered. Should I approach the camp to see what had taken place?

I thought I heard a sound. No. Yes, a sound, repetitious, over and over; galloping! It approached, and my heart rejoiced. After some time I saw Paul with Constantina. Because she was not learned in the riding of a steed, Paul held onto her, and we kept to our plan, avoiding the main roads, taking advantage of the night, traveling at full speed. We could hardly catch our breath; we could not speak; we could not even rejoice at our success. We rode and rode until the first signs of daylight began to show. We had turned south by now, and sought a place to hide until the sunlight had passed.

After tending to the horses, I went up the canyon to the thick brush under which we set up our camp. For the first time I was able to look at Constantina and pause. She was a tall woman, with dark brown hair wound around her head in the patrician style, but which had come loose and dangled down on one side. She wore a stately garment, now soiled and torn. She had brown eyes, a fine nose and long fingers. She was a beautiful woman, and had no doubt been made sport of by the soldiers of Licinius. My heart was pained in looking upon her, for she was certainly not accustomed to the conditions that she had to endure.

We had little to offer her in way of comfort, for we had traveled lightly. Paul handed her some bread, and water from the stream. She graciously accepted, because she must have been hungry. There was silence between us in all these actions; perhaps it was the tenseness of what had just occurred, together with the awkwardness of her not knowing either of us. In any case, we all sat and ate what little we had. Paul gathered some leaves for us to rest on through the day. "I am sorry, daughter of our Emperor, that we lack comforts to offer you," I said.

Then she surprised both of us when she replied, "Address me as Constantina," as she stretched out on the ground. Perhaps I had been wrong about her, for she seemed suddenly at ease, even in these harsh conditions. "You are Paul, and you are John, correct?" she asked. I bowed. "John, you, both of you, have saved my life. We have to travel as companions to safety, and look out for one another. I am so grateful, but I am too exhausted to express it now. But I do have one request: treat me as an equal as we take this journey. It will be more comfortable for you, and much more comfortable for me. Agreed?" We lifted our hands in the soldier's sign for "yes," and I lay down to rest while Paul kept the first watch. I smiled to myself. I think I will like this Constantina.

After some hours I awoke. "Take a rest now, Paul. I can watch," I said. He motioned with his hand "no" and I understood he was not yet tired. So we both watched as the daughter of the Emperor slept underneath Paul's cloak. Perhaps she became aware of neither of us sleeping, for soon Constantina awoke, and we all ate more of our precious bread.

"How were you two chosen to take such a delicate and dangerous mission?" she whispered. She appeared more rested since we arrived in this spot hours before. We paused at her question, and I pointed to Paul, as he pointed to me, smiling. She laughed at this. "I suppose you soldiers fight for glory, so that you will be remembered long after you are gone," she continued.

"Why would I care what someone thinks of me when I am dead?" Paul asked. I nudged him, for perhaps Constantina would find his brusqueness unsuitable. "I mean…" he began, to reword his comment. Constantina smiled.

"Paul, John, I insist that we speak as equals here. The titles and customs I have to endure all day are only ceremonial, and I much prefer to be a real person, and to deal with true men."

Paul began to answer her question. "We volunteered for this errand, Con…onstintinastantina." He hesitated in using simply her name, but such was her request, "for, and I do not mean to exalt ourselves, we knew we could accomplish it. Both of us know these lands; we have much battle experience, and know how soldiers think. The other reason John will tell you," he said.

"Paul loves an adventure, and will never pass up such an opportunity," I said, knowing what was in Paul's mind. "But, my love for such excitement would never supersede my judgment on whether I could accomplish a mission. I would never have volunteered if I were not certain we could get you safely home."

She looked at both of us and asked "But why two of you? Why not just you, Paul, or just you, John?"

Paul again spoke. "We have always been more successful when together. John knows my heart and I his, and when we work, we do so as one. We are stronger together."

Constantina thought for a long time, then responded, "The bond between you is enviable. Is this common within your legion?"

I looked down to reflect for a moment. There was a pause as I became confident in our new familiarity. I responded to her question with one of my own. "Have you no one with whom you feel a closeness, Con…stantina?" It was still difficult for me to address her without her title.

"I will tell you, on our way, of the life of the daughter of an Emperor, and then you can decide whether such a position is enviable or not," she said, "but now let us rest some," and she lay down again. This time Paul settled in also, and I took the watch.

*** 

By the time evening came, it began to rain. This would make our traveling more difficult, but as Paul explained to Constantina, "We will make this an advantage for ourselves, for they will never be able to pick up our trail during or after the storm. Are you up to this, my lady?" he asked.

She smiled: "My father used to laugh at the fact that my dream was not to be a queen or empress, but rather a soldier, like you. As a child I used to arm myself with a wooden sword and shield and challenge anyone who approached. I was not the most lady-like child, but I wanted to be like my father, who fought his way to his position, as you know. So for me, to set out with you now is, yes, filled with hardships, but I am living this as a fulfillment of that dream." We smiled at this, and were glad at her good will.

Because it was not yet time to depart, we settled in more, and Constantina seemed to be increasingly curious about us. She turned and asked, "What about you, Paul? Have you always wanted to be a soldier?"

Paul was usually quiet about his past, but surprised me with his candor toward her. He reflected for a moment, gazing above her head as if witnessing a scene from his past. "When I was a boy, I was raised in the countryside; I barely remember my father; I was so young when he died of sickness. He left my mother some land, but she died also, and then I was raised by an uncle. I must laugh because I too had my wooden sword and dreamed of another life, of leaving the country to join the legions. Perhaps I longed to escape the pain, perhaps I longed for excitement. When I was barely a man, I had to make a choice: try to survive on that bit of land, or join the legion. Which choice I made, well, you know."

"But" Constantina continued, "what of the future? Do you always want to be a soldier? Is this the goal that you have reached and are content with?"

Paul responded by chuckling. "It is curious how we so often end up from where we have begun. I have passed through many ordeals. I have risked my life for those I care about. I almost lost my own life more than once, I have been injured. I have seen my friends killed before my eyes. The other side of adventure, my lady, is tragedy. For this, yes, I have a goal. Once my time in the legion is completed I hope for sufficient land to have a house and a farm to sustain myself in one of the provinces. So you see, I now find myself destined for the life that I sought to escape. I do not regret my time in the legion; I love it. But when I grow older a life of peace is more compelling."

"Paul, call me Constantina," she insisted again, and to this we all smiled, for we had forgotten again to address her as an equal. She turned to me. "And what about you, John? Do you also desire to be a soldier for your entire life?"

I shook my head. "No, no. May I just say, whatever Paul just said, the same applies to me?" and we all laughed.

"It is now sufficiently dark for us to start our journey," Paul said. At this we covered ourselves as well as we could, and walked out into the cold, driving rain.

The going was difficult as we tried to make our way through the mud. We did our best to protect the Emperor's daughter, as well as ourselves, from the cold, but to no avail. Our horses moved forward with difficulty. "I hope your father does not punish us for bringing his daughter back ill and feverish to his household," I said.

"We should not stop on my account. If we are all taken ill, then we will have time to recover in Rome, with the help of the palace doctors. For now, it is our safety that matters most," she said.

"Behold John, she even thinks like a soldier," Paul said, smiling. We proceeded in this way for four or five hours, to take full advantage of the adverse weather, until we could proceed no further. We found a cave where we could rest, and also give our horses some protection. We felt it was safe enough here to recover before descending further south toward our goal.

Perhaps it was the cold, for we remained silent, too uncomfortable to sleep. I piled some dry leaves for Constantina, but she did not want to lie down just yet. It was too dangerous to light a fire to dry our clothes, so we would have to make due, and perhaps the next day would favor us with sunlight.

\*\*\*

The following day we had planned to continue our journey south. Paul left our cave and came back some minutes later, shaking his head. "We will lose the horses and perhaps ourselves too in this rain and mud. We must wait," and so we remained in that place the whole next day and night to wait for the rain to lighten. On the second day, as dawn broke and light filtered into our grotto, I could see Paul standing outside, because it was his watch. I knew him so well, I could almost read his thoughts from the strain of his muscles, and I knew that he was on alert. I crept silently out toward him. Constantina slept.

"What is it?" I asked him, more with my gestures than words. Paul motioned to his ear, and we both listened. There was a rustling coming from above us, where there was a road at the lip of the valley where we were hidden. Paul motioned that he would go up, but I grabbed his arm, and made him understand with my gestures that I should go, because I knew this terrain. He relented, and went back to rouse Constantina, to prepare for any trouble.

I used the brush and trees as cover, but had to be extremely careful to make no noise as I climbed up the valley toward a rhythmic sound, which seemed to be a soldier's step, but I was not yet sure. I approached more closely, very slowly, until I could distinguish a horse and its rider, walking side by side, on the road above. If this was an isolated soldier of Licinius, who had come across our trail, I would have to kill him for the protection of the Emperor's daughter. I hoped it was simply one who was passing through, so that we could remain hidden, and not risk revealing our presence. This could also be a trap to draw us out, with others waiting and watching. I would have to anticipate any of the enemy's plans.

I approached the road until I could actually see him, dressed in soldier's attire, and with the insignia of Licinius. As I spent some time observing him, I came to the conclusion that their Commander had sent out scouts in many directions, this being one of them. He was not following any apparent trail, but was probably told to go south before turning east or west, and to report back on his findings. We could let him go on his way, I thought, for if we waited for the cover of night, we could avoid him altogether. These were my thoughts when, in the distance, I heard one of our horses neigh. The soldier turned suddenly, patted his horse, and listened intently. I was sure that Paul, at that moment, was feverishly working to calm our horses. I stood with my hand on my sword while sweat ran down my back.

This soldier proceeded to tie his horse to a tree and began to creep off the road, down into the direction of our camp. I was well hidden, about 150 paces from him. I could not let him reach our camp alive. This was certain. I let him climb some distance down the hill first, so that I would have the advantage. If he were a man, he would turn to fight me; if he lost courage, he would run down the hill, where Paul would cut him off. He made excessive noise as he made his way down, apparently unaccustomed to such terrain. I was able to approach within 50 paces unnoticed, at which point I removed my sword from its sheath and made the enemy aware of my presence.

He turned in surprise, but swiftly drew his sword and leapt before me to engage me in battle. Because he did not call for help, I knew he was isolated, and by eliminating him we could take flight immediately in relative safety, or so I hoped.

I was practiced at combat; my adversary was younger and probably less experienced, but he hurtled toward me with a vengeance. Both he and I were without shields, finding them encumbering in our stealth. I engaged him, and we landed swords repeatedly; he was strong, but I was more so. He slammed his sword repeatedly toward me, but I successfully blocked him with my sword, and evaded him with my swiftness. I endeavored to keep on the higher ground to prevent him from taking the advantage. I would keep him off balance and allow him to swing at me. His anger grew as he missed again and again. I was not attempting to slash at him until I assessed his strength and skill. His fear and fury would be his undoing, so I allowed his rage to grow. We were now in combat on equal footing. He continued to slash and fail. Then I, calculating his slowness and drawing his rage and his sword to my right side, plunged mine into his chest, and a great river of his blood burst forth, as if I had punctured the walls of a cistern. He cried out, but my sword went deep. His cries ceased as his blood continued to bubble forth from his limp body, lying prostrate under the forest canopy. I dragged him under some of the undergrowth so that it would be some time before he was discovered. My duty completed, I returned to our camp, puffing for breath, trembling from battle.

When I returned, Paul and Constantina looked horrified; I did not know why until I looked down and saw my tunic soaked in blood. "I am well. It is his blood," pointing my sword up the hill. They rejoiced, but refrained from embracing me, due to the blood.

We decided to push forward in daylight, trusting my instincts that this was a lone spy, and the others were far from here. We were eager to get Constantina into safer territory. I went down to the stream, however, to wash my soaked tunic. As I did so, I heard Paul approach from behind and sit down beside me. I said, "Blood flows so easily in the Empire. One day ours will flow also."

Paul looked at me curiously and asked, "Why do you speak such words, John? We are soldiers; that is our task." He paused. "Do you think our lives will end in this way, brother?" I stopped scrubbing and turned to him:

"While I was in Egypt and my mother was ailing, I began to wonder about death. Until that point, I had always seen it as a matter of course, something which simply happens and is to be accepted, as every soldier should. But as I received news that her health was failing, and that I would not be able to return to Rome, a longing was born in me, a longing to see her once more, to share with her the events and thoughts and feelings that she had no knowledge of. I prayed much to Mithras to protect my mother, my sister, and you, Paul, that we might see one another in this life, and also be united in Hades. I wondered whether our bonds with one another endure, if they are even stronger than death. I do not regret killing this soldier; it was my duty, and there was no other way to guarantee our safety. But I wonder if he had that hope that death would somehow be the beginning of something good, if he looked forward to being with someone whom he loved. He lost his life so easily, when he least expected it, just doing his duty. I wonder sometimes if it will be the same with us." I paused and smiled. "These are my strange thoughts, Paul," I said, as we rose to climb back up the hill. Paul patted me between the shoulders and was silent. This was the nature of our relationship; he did not have to respond, and often our silences together spoke more than many words.

We still had several days ahead of us before reaching Roman territory, and we changed our course in case the soldier's not returning provoked a search through the area we had lodged in. Though changing course would prolong our trip even more, it was the safest thing to do. Our time in the legion had taught us to follow our instincts in these matters.

Mercifully, it grew somewhat warmer, but we could see that Constantina was growing fatigued as we pressed on. She was not one to complain, but I observed the signs of her weariness. "Let us rest here," Paul said, when the strain of the journey became apparent on her face. On the fourth day after our encounter with the soldier of Licinius, we heard a horse further down from us, on the road. This time Paul took charge of approaching the sound with stealth, sword drawn. We stopped and calmed our horses to prevent any sign of our presence. It seemed a long time before I heard Paul's signal for us to continue. It would be strange for an enemy soldier to be this far south, but one could never know due to the coming conflict. Once I heard his whistle, we approached the clearing and came upon Paul and another soldier who was a scout looking for us. He bowed when he saw the daughter of our Emperor, and Constantina acknowledged him.

"I have been ordered to bring you safely back to our camp, which is but half a day distance from here. We are to keep your arrival in camp discreet, my lady, because we do not have word of the troop movements of our enemy. If news travels to him that you are here, you could be in danger. We will bring you veiled into camp, directly into a tent arranged for you, where you will rest the night, before we descend down to Rome. And you," he continued, referring to Paul and me, "are to accompany us before returning to your duty in Germania,". Our orders were clear, so we began our trek toward greater safety.

We were led to the edge of the military camp, and into a large tent on the outskirts, where we were told to wait for the Commander. Shortly thereafter, a short and stout, middle aged man entered smiling, and very happy to see Constantina and us.

"Bring some hot broth," he ordered his men, "and some hot water also, for them to wash." He bowed to the daughter of the Emperor, and apologized for the humble accommodations. Constantina graciously thanked him as he motioned us to sit. "I know you are all wearied, so I will not inquire of the details of your journey. I want to be of service to you before you resume your passage," he continued. "We will send word to Rome that you are safely with us, my lady, and when your escort arrives you can continue your descent. These men who have undertaken your rescue will rest here and then return to Germania, where they will receive due recognition for their task by their Commander. These are my orders. In the meantime, I would ask you not to leave this tent, because we want your presence to be a secret. These men will take up residence with the other soldiers. If I may be of any other service," he began, rising, "simply let my guard know of your needs."

Before he could leave, Constantina rose, in the full dignity of her status as the daughter of the one we serve. "I do have several requirements," she began. "These men will be as my Praetorian, and will accompany me to Rome. They have kept me safe this far, and I will continue to entrust myself to them. I will descend to Rome, not when the escort arrives, but when I feel fit for the journey, because my entrance into the city might cause much commotion, and may be taxing for me in this state. My father himself will express his gratitude to these men in Rome, I can assure you. I would also like them not to be housed with the other soldiers, but next to me, so that they may continue to safeguard me even here. I will not entrust myself to others, given what has taken place." The Commander seemed confused, not accustomed to a woman changing his orders, yet perceiving that her authority was greater than his, he complied. "Thank you, Commander, you may go," she said, dismissing him.

Constantina motioned us to sit with her, and we all drank eagerly of the hot broth, having consumed only old bread and stream water for over a week. Paul and I were unsure how to address her now, because we had grown accustomed to her as our equal, and we now witnessed her as one with authority. She soon set us at our ease as more hot food was brought and the wine began to flow. It seemed a feast, and we did indeed celebrate our victory over the circumstances which we had faced. We ate and talked of our travels for some time, until it began to grow dark. Two soldiers had been assigned outside her quarters, sworn to secrecy. They brought in lamps. "Do you object to accompanying me to Rome, to be like my Praetorian for the journey?" she asked.

Perhaps we had much wine, for Paul and I burst out, "Praetorian, no!"

Constantina laughed. "Oh yes, I forgot you detest the Praetorian. They were a bit like walking statues, were they not? Intelligence was never one of their gifts. You must be pleased that they were disbanded."

Paul and I agreed. "To accompany you to Rome, my lady, is something we are grateful to you for asking. Whenever you need us, we are at your service," I stated.

As the evening grew on, our conversation grew more personal. Constantina asked again about our families and friends. Because they were like our brothers, we told her of Crispus and Crispinianus who were still in Ostia. Paul asked her to tell us of her father, our glorious Emperor.

"Most think that my adventuresome spirit comes from my

father, but I actually take after my grandmother most of all. Oh, my father does not avoid risk for the sake of the Empire, or whatever goal he might be seeking, but he is, at heart, a soldier, perhaps like you. He is disciplined and driven by duty most of all. My grandmother is the one who has fed me her dreams to live other lives, to seek out other peoples, to see other lands, to go beyond the limits that my state might impose, while preserving its decorum. So if you ask me about my father, I can simply say he is one who is dedicated and loyal to those he cares about. Outside of that, his duty is to the Empire, and for this he works and sacrifices and dreams and plans. You would not believe some of the dreams that he has, but I dare not discuss that, despite the comfort we have found with one another."

There was a long pause, then Constantina took up the questioning. "I can see that your bond with each other is strong, firmer than I have ever seen among soldiers before. Are you bound to one another in the way of the Greeks?"

Paul gazed at her and replied, "The bond between us is greater than Greek or Roman," She smiled at this, and some time passed before anyone spoke. I dared to ask, "And you Constantina, to whom are you bound?" Looking back at this conversation, I know not how I dared address her with such familiarity.

"I have not your freedom to decide to whom I may give my heart. I will marry the one whom my parents decide. Whether I will love him, or he will love me, is another matter. That, my friends, is my duty. So perhaps we are not so unalike," she said.

"What would you like to do, if you had your way?" Paul asked.

"I would remain here several days to rest, then I would take those horses outside, and I would ride with both of you east, where none may know me. There we would join a legion in the provinces, seeking adventure and glory along the way. When we tired of that legion, we would join another, so that our lives would rival the journeys of Odysseus." Paul laughed.

"But you have forgotten one matter, Constantina! You are a woman!" and we all laughed.

"Perhaps I can remedy that," she said, as she took a helmet and put her hair underneath it. We again laughed at the thought. These were her dreams. What harm can be in dreams?

That next day Constantina fell ill, due to the cold and rain, and we ended up remaining in that camp six days until she recovered her strength for the journey to Rome. Her father, our glorious Emperor, had sent her word that he would meet her there as soon as he was able to free himself from the turmoil in the north. He also sent word that Paul and I were to await his return. By the sixth day we all felt considerably better, and readied ourselves for the final leg of the journey. The escort from Rome had arrived, but Constantina put them in a subordinate position in our entourage. In all, one hundred soldiers would accompany us on our journey, so that, in the unlikely event that the troops of Licinius would track us this far, they would have a formidable task in opposing our forces. Constantina was able to travel in a carriage, with Paul and me riding beside her.

We traveled in this way for some days, until a delegation met us, consisting of senators and the palace guard. We learned that there was much celebration for the return of Constantina to the city, and many wanted to share in both the joy and the glory associated with her rescue. Because Paul and I were soldiers, due to protocol we dropped back in the procession, for it was customary that senators be first, followed by the palace guard, then the others, depending on rank. After some minutes, a message was sent to us. Constantina requested that we ride next to her, side by side, into the city. We approached her carriage, passing the frowning guards. This was an honor, and she smiled on us as we took our places.

By the time we entered Rome, it seemed that the entire city had come out to greet us. As we advanced, there was celebration and song, clapping, and dancing by all the citizens. Our brother soldiers also came out to observe, and saluted Paul and me in particular, offering congratulations. "Paul! John!" we heard from among the legionaries. There were Crispus and Crispinianus, not shipped out from Rome yet, waving and greeting us. Even Fulvia and the children came out to see us, though I only learned of this the next day, due to the large numbers. Constantina saluted the crowds, and the procession went on for hours. "My lady," I leaned in and asked her, "Why not head directly to the palace, because you are tired from the journey?" She replied that she would not disappoint the crowds.

"This is Rome, John, and we must respect her," were her words. We continued on for some time, until she reached her lodgings.

"Worthy soldiers and friends," she addressed us once we were inside, "Take your leave now. I will call you to return so we may speak." We made our way to our quarters to rest. Not sure when we would return to our men, we sent word to our Commander that we were under orders to remain in Rome for some days. In this way, one adventure was ended, as another was about to begin.

# Chapter 5: In the Eye of the Emperor

"What do you think is going to happen to both of you now?" asked Fulvia the next day as she visited us in our barracks.

"You sound as if we were about to be punished!" I teased her.

She persisted. "Do you think you will meet the Emperor?"

Paul shook his head. "We are just soldiers, carrying out a mission. I believe we will be honored for a day by the Roman magistrates, perhaps even by the Senate, then return to our duties. I will be happy if that is the case. Then we can rejoin our men."

By the time my sister departed, it was dark, but the lights of Rome surrounded us and filled the streets. It was good to be back again. Although I would not hesitate to do my duty in Germania, I was content to be back in Rome, a place which I had become accustomed to and now considered to be my home.

"Thank you, brother, for your courage and strength," Paul said, breaking the silence. I felt much gratitude toward him also, but there was no need to express it in words. We continued to look out on the city as it slowly darkened and the silence grew.

Before retiring, both Paul and I sorted through our supplies, assessing what we would need to replace for our journey back to

Germania. We decided to make arrangements so that we might travel with the garrison of Crispus and Crispinianus, and enjoy their companionship along the way. The next day we resolved to finalize these preparations.

***

Having obtained the necessary supplies, and spoken with the local commanders about our assignment in the north, we simply had to await our orders. Over a week had passed when we were called to the quarters of our Commander. Upon entering, he saluted us and handed us a written message. Before we could read it he explained, "The Emperor has called you to report to the palace tomorrow. I am happy for you, men." We were stunned. He saluted us, and we returned to our barracks.

Fulvia had been anxious about our future, so I sent word to her of the message. Within an hour, she, Crispus, and Crispinianus appeared. Our lodgings were humble, being within the garrison, but we had a soldier's feast with olives, bread, *garum*[28], and wine. We used the occasion not only to rejoice at our meeting with the Emperor, but also to celebrate our safe return to Rome, and the success of our mission. The next day we resolved to make a sacrifice to Mithras for our triumph. When night fell, Fulvia returned home to care for her children, but we were joined by other friends in the garrison who continued to celebrate with us after most had retired.

***

The anticipation of our meeting with the Emperor gave neither Paul nor me any rest that night. We were to appear at his palace at midday, but we were both dressed and ready by sunrise. Our friends had gathered around us also, congratulating

---

[28] A fermented fish sauce popular among Romans.

us on the privilege of meeting the Emperor himself. Several came to me asking that I convey messages to Constantine concerning the loyalty of our soldiers. The Commander of the local garrison came to us, in fact, and congratulated us for the mission.

I had a mixture of emotions that morning: gratitude, excitement, anticipation, nervousness. But I put on my soldier's face, showing no sentiment at all, and met Paul at the bottom of the hill. At the appointed hour we made our way across the city, into the main Forum, and toward the Palatine[29]. Many turned and asked one another why two fully equipped soldiers were in the Forum at that hour, but we did not want to create a stir, so we proceeded quickly through the crowds.

In our walks across the city, both Paul and I had seen the outside of the Emperor's residence numerous times, but it now seemed larger than before, almost ominous, for the power it represented was great. We began ascending the many white marble stairs, passing dozens of guards, and making our way toward the entrance. The central bronze doors were three times the height of Paul, covered in battle scenes of Roman triumphs. The entire structure was beautiful, for those who have never seen it, covered in white marble with green columns, rising higher with each step that took us closer. By the time we reached the first landing, we felt quite small. There were about thirty guards on duty at the entrance. As we continued our ascent, two men approached us and motioned for us to stop. We were approached by a stern soldier who demanded our names.

"I am John."

"I am Paul."

Hearing this, the guards immediately became our servants, rather than our masters. Paul gave me a look to indicate his amusement.

---

[29] The Palatine hill in Rome was the location of the palace of the Emperor. It overlooks the Roman Forum.

The bronze doors were opened to admit us, and we stepped inside to witness even more marvels than outside. We found ourselves within a walled garden; in the center was a large pool with a flowing fountain. This was surrounded by life-sized statues of the Emperors, and rows of plants that I had never seen before, with flowers and fruits of strange shapes and colors. It was a garden of calm and peace, which was not what I expected as soon as I stepped into the palace.

I had imagined the interior of the Emperor's residence to be somewhat severe, resembling the dwelling of a general. I had in my mind the image of a dimly lit room with figures on the walls of Rome's enemies being conquered. Instead, my breath was taken away when we were ushered into an inner chamber, which was apparently an official meeting place. Rather than darkness, the room was filled with light, due to the large windows on all sides. The walls and floors were covered with a stone with a pink hue, which transformed the entire hall into a warm and glowing jewel. There was no furniture; it was as if the light that filled the room made it unnecessary. From the windows, I could hear the crowds in the Forum below, but they were a world away from what was before us. The walls and floors gleamed, and reflected the light in patterns on the facing walls. There were several more statues of the Emperors on the far side, next to a large, bronze door, at which two guards were stationed. I know not how much time passed before the door began to open.

The palace guard entered and announced the approach of the Emperor. Paul and I stood at attention as a large, powerfully-built man entered the room, dressed in a toga, with arms stretched out toward us. Constantine was clean shaven, handsome, with a square jaw, round eyes, and a neck as strong as a bull. We bowed before him, but he came directly up to us and embraced us like brothers. Perhaps he sensed our nervousness, because he quickly set us at ease. He motioned us to follow him, and we crossed the room to that window overlooking all of Rome below.

The Emperor began, "Be at ease, men. I am a soldier also. What you have done for my daughter, you have done for me, and I do not know how to express my gratitude for saving the life of my beloved. Tell me about yourselves: your families, how long you have been in the legion, what your hopes are." I recounted to him our humble backgrounds, Paul and I both being raised on farms and both, without knowing each other, dreaming of entering the legion. We spoke of our parents, and I of Fulvia. Paul had no living family. I told him of our meeting each other in Germania and our success there, the bond that formed between us, and of my being sent to Egypt.

"What are your plans for your future?" he asked.

Paul replied, "They are those of every soldier: to complete our military duty and obtain sufficient land to have a home, and perhaps a farm for support, either here or in one of the provinces."

"You seek not to use your fame within the web of Roman politics?" he asked. Paul and I smiled, for this would be the last thing we would want.

"A home and peace would be sufficient, for we have fought many battles, and once our turn in the legion is complete, I for one, would not seek to fight more." The Emperor paused and looked out over the city for a long time.

I looked at him more closely. Constantine seemed more soldier than Emperor, and I respected him for this. "Constantina has grown fond of you and tells me that she would have you live close to the palace, so that she will always know that you are near when she is in Rome. She has also requested that you, and only you, be her personal escort, should she need to call on you. But giving you one task to replace another is not a reward, for I wish to express my gratitude to you for saving my daughter from the villain Licinius. How can I recompense you for giving me my daughter?" He looked at us as he said these words, but neither of us knew what to say. "You have said it yourself: you want to retire with some land as income. Because Constantina has also expressed her desire, I will satisfy all of you. I will anticipate your retirement, giving you a home so that you can live in comfort, close to the palace, in a location that has come into my possession on the Caelian hill. I will also bequest to you land, which is already being farmed and is leased out, to serve as your income. Though the house is not yet complete, I will have workmen ready it for you. I wish to express my gratitude by making your life not one of sacrifice, but of reward. And I have instructed Constantina, if she ever has need of you, to call upon you." He paused and looked at us with the dignity befitting an Emperor. "Is this acceptable?" Both of us were speechless, but managed to answer affirmatively. The Emperor then embraced us and walked out the door, turning before he left and said, "My daughter awaits you," motioning to another exit.

The guard led us through innumerable corridors and statues to another large room where Constantina was waiting. As soon as we entered, Paul burst out, "Constantina!" and went as if to embrace her.

But she motioned with her head to the guard present, and said in a low voice, "We must keep to the formalities as long as they are here."

At that point, we both bowed and greeted her, "My lady." She smiled and motioned us to sit at a table covered with fresh wine and honey, sweet cakes made of dates, another of pears, and many other fruits. The servants poured wine into our glasses and handed us our plates, but we had scant appetite at that moment.

"Are you content with the decision that my father has made?" she asked. We were still in a daze, for it was so unexpected, and our lives were about to change in unknown ways. "Will you miss being in the legion, being sent to the provinces to battle enemies and seek adventure?" she asked.

Paul answered, "No," and she laughed.

"But Paul, you are the one who is always ready to run off to seek excitement. For this I was unsure of my father's solution.

Was I wrong?"

Paul looked at her and thought, then answered, "I have seen too many of my friends perish; I have seen John in great danger; I have followed the orders of others my entire life. None of this I will miss. And if I feel a need for adventure, I will go to the races. And I will bring you also!" he said, and Constantina laughed long and hard at this. Having agreed that she would call on us when she was next in Rome, we bid her farewell.

\*\*\*

Paul and I were silent as we left the palace and descended the many stairs. It would take time to understand the consequences of what had just occurred. As we looked up, we heard "Brothers!" and found our Maltese friends, Crispus and Crispinianus, at the bottom of the steps. They looked so small from above, seeming shorter of stature, but they were formidable men when up close. They were smiling and excited, as they were anticipating news from us, but neither Paul nor I knew where to begin. "We have come to escort you back to your quarters, sirs," Crispinianus said, jokingly saluting us.

We laughed as Crispus broke in. "Tell us!" We began to walk as we recounted the whole turn of events. Crispus grew more and more excited, and started to jump up and down right there in the middle of the street! Paul laughed, then suggested that we return to our dwellings to continue our discussion, so as not to become a spectacle in front of the Emperor's gate.

Within minutes, Fulvia arrived. How did she always receive the news about what was happening in our lives before anyone else? I do not know. She began to cry. Crispus and Crispinianus were shouting and jumping, and soon half our garrison was present. Before we knew it, they had picked up Paul and me, and we were being paraded around the barracks, with much singing and celebration. Our friends, and even those who knew us less, all celebrated the turn our lives had taken.

Even the Commander came out when he heard the news. "You deserve this, and more. You are good men!" he said, congratulating us in front of all present. The celebration lasted all that day.

When it was fully dark, and many had to leave to attend to their duties, Fulvia insisted that we make our way up the Caelian hill to locate the dwelling which would be ours. So we crossed the city once more and found the hill. and then the street. "Look how close you will be to the Emperor's palace!" Fulvia exclaimed. Indeed, it was a stone's throw away. We made our way up the road and encountered a group of soldiers descending. We would later learn that there was a garrison at the top of that very hill. Soon we came upon the house.

The home was built out of what appeared to be an *insula*, or apartment house, with shops below that had been walled up. Some windows were uncovered, but because it was dark, it was difficult to see inside. Those walls we did see were bare, and some of the floors were unfinished. It was a very large edifice, in any case. As we walked slowly down the hill, we noticed that the area was the site of many large, luxurious homes, and we felt privileged to be given such a dwelling.

It was difficult to sleep that night due to all that had occurred earlier. Even though it was very late by the time I lay down, I gazed at the full moon for a long time, giving thanks to the gods for the good things that were occurring. When it was a little past dawn, Paul was already up and anxious to begin our new day. We made our way to the Caelian hill to view the home in daylight. On our arrival, we could hear that workmen were already present, obviously on orders from the Emperor to complete the work as soon as possible. As the door was ajar, we walked in. "You must be John and Paul," a dark-haired, middle-aged man approached and greeted us, bowing. "I am Gallicanus, your servant." We were not aware that the house came with a slave, and the surprise must have shown on our faces. We had never had a slave before. Having one now seemed awkward. We were accustomed to following orders and carrying out the missions entrusted to us. We were comfortable taking care of ourselves, whether in the field or at home. I was unsure of the usefulness of such a one. "May I show you your home?" he asked. Gallicanus led us through the unusual layout of the building, which was really at least two separate edifices which had been united. He then took us down to a subterranean level which, he said, could be the wine cellar. "I have experience in the purchasing and keeping of wines," he explained. "This cellar would be perfect, and I can keep your wines, oils, and *garum* here." We agreed, and marveled at the layout of such a grand place. "These used to be the shops, facing the street," he explained as we ascended once more to ground level. "They are now small rooms which can be used for storage, or guest quarters, or whatever else you please. Simply tell the men working what you want them to do here."

Paul and I had the same thought as we said, "Guest quarters," for we were thinking of our friends who would still have many years in the legion. We could share our good fortune by giving them a place of respite in Rome.

We were happy with the edifice, but had little idea of how to instruct the workmen. I knew that a meeting with my sister was in order.

"It is an odd building," she said, as we walked through the next day. "Let us decide on which areas will be for living, which for guests, and which for storage. Then I can direct the workmen accordingly." I knew she would be happy to take on this task for us, and Paul and I were most willing to hand it to her, because we knew little of these things.

"Greetings, my lady," Gallicanus said as we entered the lower part of the building. We introduced our slave to Fulvia. It still felt awkward to have a man as our slave, and I asked my sister about this.

"Treat them well and they will treat you better," she stated. Because her husband had an important position, she had some experience with slaves.

Paul, Fulvia, and I were all from the country, and enjoyed the open spaces we had grown up in. In our new home we wished to have a garden area, but there was no plot of earth available. There was an enclosed courtyard in the center of the edifice from which the roof could be removed, and a garden could be planted. Fulvia again offered to direct the design and construction of the courtyard, and we again readily agreed. "Yours is a home in the city, but it will seem you are in the country, on a farm or a vast garden, for everywhere you look you will find the themes of nature, which will lift your spirits," she said. Once these decisions had been made she met with the workmen and gave specific directions on finishing the structure.

My sister was also fond of the theatre, and asked if she could decorate a large room with scenes from the stage. "Perhaps we could host plays and readings and music here!" she said enthusiastically. Though we had rarely gone to the theatre, we both nodded agreement to her. I much preferred the races or combat as a spectacle, but did not necessarily want these themes on the walls of our home. Fulvia had clearer ideas on bringing the structure to life, so we surrendered to her judgment.

"Please do not go into the courtyard the men are constructing," she said to us that next week, "until it is complete." Fulvia had insisted on keeping the courtyard a secret from us as the workers were coming and going. We could hear much construction taking place, as pipes were laid, cement was poured, and artists were called in. I was curious as to what my sister was doing, but promised her not to inquire.

"I made no promise to your sister," Crispus said, as he slipped beyond the covering to view the work taking place inside. He emerged wide eyed. "Whatever it will be, it is a major work. I will tell you no more." Fulvia must have had at least fifteen men working on the courtyard, and she was often there, with her children, to supervise.

When the garden area was completed a few weeks later, my

sister led us in. As we approached, we heard water running; on entering, we beheld my sister's creation: An open space filled with flowers and plants in pots, covered with glistening marble all around except for one wall, on which there was a beautiful fresco and an elaborate fountain below. We were speechless. Crispus and Crispinianus were present to witness the unveiling. "It is beautiful, Fulvia. Where did you find your inspiration for such a paradise?" Paul asked.

She looked proudly on us all and began, "I wanted you to have a place to lift your spirits, just as Spring lifts the sunken spirits of the world after a long winter." We all approached the fresco and peered at it more closely.

"What does it mean?" Crispus asked her.

"In the middle is Persephone, having returned to her mother Demeter, bringing the new life of Spring with her. On her other side is Bacchus, rejoicing with her as he gives her to drink. All around there is celebration that Spring has returned, that Demeter, Persephone, and Bacchus are united, that all is well." We applauded her creation. But suddenly I noticed a detail which riveted me. I approached to take a closer look.

"Sister" I said, "is that not your pearl necklace that Persephone is wearing?

My sister smiled and continued, "Brother, if you look closely, you will see something of a family portrait. Yes, I had the painter use my face as Persephone. Now who else do you see?" I looked more closely as I recognized a resemblance to our dear mother in the face and attire of Demeter.

Then Paul broke in, "Behold, John is Bacchus!" It was true; Fulvia had told the painter to study me in the preceding days, and he had produced my likeness as Bacchus.

"Your sister has made you gods!" Crispus exclaimed. We laughed heartily, but were also moved that Fulvia had accomplished two things: she had captured the joy of the return of Spring, and she had created a portrait of our family.

"But where is Paul?" Crispus asked.

Fulvia answered, "Paul actually gave me the idea. It is the joy of your return, John, that is celebrated. Paul did not know what form his idea would take, so he may be surprised also." She paused, then smiled. "I am not finished, however. I have yet to reveal how I will immortalize Paul in other rooms." We all raised our eyebrows and looked at Paul. He shrugged, and we laughed.

Gallicanus entered, bringing wine and refreshment for our guests. He gazed at the figure of Bacchus and then at me, seeing the resemblance at once. We invited him to join us. There we sat in that cool spot for a long time, surrounded by the plants swaying in the breeze, listening to the bubbling water of the four fountains falling into basins. It was good to be here, surrounded by those I loved.

Our home was complete. Our days had been transformed.

# Chapter 6: Beginnings

T he thirst for power ran through Rome like its aqueducts, and soon Paul and I, on different occasions, were invited to swim in its current. In my case, it was Gaius Byzantius, my brother in law, who approached me.

"John, you are a good man, and have won respect in the legion as well as from the citizens of Rome. This is your year of triumph, when everyone speaks of your bravery. It is also known that you are favored by the Emperor. Why not use this fame to serve the people of Rome in a non-military way?"

I told him again of my lack of interest, even repugnance, for the political world.

"May I at least introduce you to some friends?" At his insistence, more for the sake of Fulvia, I accepted, and he invited me on several occasions to gatherings which included senators and other leaders of the people. He also extended the invitation to Paul, who also felt obliged to accept out of deference to his office. Fulvia, Paul, and I found ourselves to be disinterested participants at these occasions. We bargained with one another that we would attend a few times in order to please Gaius, then politely make him understand that we were grateful, but not interested. Fulvia detested these gatherings, but when Paul appeared, the three of us decided to have our own feast, and we would stay together so as to enjoy one another's company. Almost accidentally, we eventually made several friends among the senators. Perhaps it was because we were the only ones present without political interest. Perhaps it was because we were the only ones laughing and enjoying ourselves among the solemn crowd. In the end, I was content that we participated, for we found that not all those in the Senate were conniving, and actually remain friends with some of those men to this day.

At another time, Paul was approached at the baths by one Roman politician who asked him if he would be interested in becoming a commander. "Such a position awaits you if you are so inclined," he stated. The politician in question tried to convince Paul of the service he could render to the Empire. It was clear that there was some benefit for himself that he would not reveal. Paul, who is even less tactful than I, simply laughed and walked away.

We were soldiers, we had always been soldiers, and as simple men, we desired only to take joy in what we had been given. This baffled some of those we met, just as the thirst for power among many of Rome's elite perplexed us.

\*\*\*

When Constantina was in Rome the following year, she kept her promise and called on us. My sister was certain we were about to be given some responsibility, or that we would unwillingly be sucked into the web of Roman politics.

"Certainly you are about to receive an imperial appointment," Fulvia commented. Paul groaned. By this time we had settled into our new life, and were finding the continual offers for a political career annoying.

The next day we did report to the daughter of our Emperor. Her invitation was not to coerce us into some political office. "Would you escort me on a short journey south I must take?" We readily accepted, and soon we were accompanying her on several such journeys. She still regarded Paul and me with great affection, as we did her, and when we managed to be alone, she dropped all the customs associated with her position and treated us as brothers.

On one such excursion she asked Paul, "Is the Senate pressuring you to serve the Roman people in some public way?"

With his eyes, he made her understand "yes" but "not interested" at the same time.

"Why not?" she inquired.

"Because I do not desire more than I have been given. I have peace. Why should I seek something else?"

She nodded and replied, "I agree with you, Paul. Public life is admirable if it is indeed to serve the people. But if it were up to me, I would avoid it at all costs. There are those who are disposed to sacrifice everything, even their own happiness, to serve the cause of Rome. Others are obliged to do so. Should you ever be tempted, remember this. It is a difficult path, not always leading to happiness." She seemed saddened at the words that she imparted to us.

Because our friendship and familiarity had grown, I took her hand and, looking into her eyes, asked her, "How are you, my friend?" At this she began to weep.

We were far from Rome, the other soldiers were stationed at some distance, and we were within the tent prepared for her. It saddened Paul and me to see her in such a state.

Paul, always ready to defend those he cares about, sat next to her and asked, "Has someone injured you, my lady?" He would have taken his horse at that moment to seek out such a one and dispose of him.

But she replied "No, no one has injured me. I am sorry for this scene." She composed herself and continued, "I serve the Roman people through duty, not choice. So my life is decided by others. There seems to be so little room for happiness in such an existence. Would that I could take these horses and ride with you until the end of the Empire, and then begin to live our adventure I dreamed about on our first journey together!" She smiled and paused, then continued, "I am sorry my friends. Sometimes the pressures of my position seem too much, and there are few I can unburden myself with. I am grateful that I can do so with you."

Paul proposed to her, "Why do you not come and visit, even stay with us? We can disguise you, say you are a relative visiting. There you can take some rest."

Constantina laughed. "You know these Romans, Paul. They will claim that I have taken you both as lovers, that I bear your children, that I am conspiring against my father with you, or any other such nonsense. I am afraid my position limits my freedom. But I will always find ways to see you, my dear brothers."

As evening wore on, with the three of us gathered before a fire, we opened our hearts to one another. "Tell me more," Constantina began, "of what binds you together."

I glanced over at Paul, who continued to gaze into the flames. I started to answer her question. "It is as if, for me, between myself and others, there is always a space unfilled. With Paul, there is not this space."

There was a silence, and she turned to Paul, about to speak, then stopped herself. She addressed me instead. "From the tears in Paul's eyes, I would say that it is the same for him." At this, she leaned over and kissed Paul, and then me, on the forehead. We bid one another good night, and continued our journey the next day.

***

Politics were far from my mind when we returned to Rome, as I thought of Constantina and her sorrow. Her turmoil actually reminded me of Merytre, and of the sufferings she was to endure. Though I felt powerless to help either, I finally sat down to write my friend in Alexandria.

*Merytre,*

*With joy and sorrow I received your communication. I did not write sooner because I was at a loss. I was saddened that I was unable to see you after your father intervened, and when I received orders to return to Rome, I did not feel free to come to see you, for I was unwilling to risk your falling into your father's disfavor.*

*Your words are true. Doing one's duty is for all, but perhaps I was thinking that joy is not only for a few, but is also for all, but in differing doses and differing times.*

*I felt that joy when I received your letter. I still recall that night we walked through your beautiful city, when the buildings and the waves glowed with the light of the brightest moon I had ever seen. The joy I felt, and feel, is the realization that, when I think of Egypt, I think of you; you are the face of Egypt for me, Merytre, and always will be. Is that not cause for joy?*

*I will always remember you, and always wish you happiness, in whatever doses and times the gods may dispense it.*

*John*

For the present I was partaking of a great joy, and this made me more sorrowful for those who had only duty to guide them.

# Chapter 7: Something More

Neither Paul nor I were accustomed to having much leisure time. In the past, our military obligations had always occupied us, and we had considered ourselves lucky if we were able to attend a gladiatorial game in the provinces, or have more than a day of rest at a time. In our new life, we had no responsibilities except those that we set for ourselves. We did indeed keep much of the discipline we had learned in the legion; in fact, we regularly participated in the exercises of the nearby garrison to maintain our battle skills, should Constantina call on us.

We began attending the games in Rome. Races had replaced gladiatorial combat. Paul, Crispus, and Crispinianus (after their return to Ostia), and I could be found often cheering the chariot of our choice. The competition of the games reminded us of the competition in battle. Instead of swords, there were steeds and wheels; with some force of imagination, we could transform all chariots, except our chosen one, into the enemy. Paul was the most passionate of all of us, sometimes going to the races by himself when the rest of us were otherwise occupied.

"Off to the races, back before sunset," he called out one day as he made his way to the Circus. On one particular occasion, it was well after dark, and he had still not returned. Because this was unlike Paul, I began to walk in the direction of the races.

"There you are!" I said, as I came upon him after some time.

As I approached I was surprised to see his face covered with blood, with an open wound above his eye. "What happened?" I asked, as I came closer. With his fist, he made me understand that he had been involved in a fight. "Are you injured?" I asked.

"Not as much as the other!" he replied. I could be an irascible person, but Paul even more so.

Besides the races and the time spent with our friends, the absence of obligations led me to reflect more on matters of the heart. When my life was filled with activities, I had not the presence of mind to seek the meaning of events or people, and I had rarely thought of these matters at all until my time of need in Egypt. Soon in Rome, these unanswered questions returned to haunt me.

One evening when my sister was present, after a meal prepared by Gallicanus, I began to recount to Fulvia my stay in Egypt and my meeting with Merytre. "I thought you were going to marry her!" Paul interjected, laughing.

"She was indeed a beautiful woman, but that was not what I was seeking. In my friendship with her, I began to understand the way her people see life and death, and it made me wonder about my own. I haven't thought much about her words since then, but I wonder now if there lies some truth in them." Fulvia insisted I tell them more, so I continued. "She explained how this life is a preparation for the next one. Once dead, their loved ones live on, not as shadows, but continue just as they did before. The body continues its uses in the beyond." Paul smiled. "I knew not what to think of these things. When I received the news that my mother had died, I wanted to believe that I would see her once more, not only as a shadow, but as she was, as if I could come visit her at your home, Fulvia. I wanted it to be so. I devoted myself even more to Mithras for protection for those I hold in my heart, both alive and dead. And he must have heard at least part of my prayer, for behold, I am here, and you are here also." The air was thick with reflection, and there was a silence. I continued, "I was lonely in Alexandria, and that solitude made me think deeply on these things. Sometimes those questions from the land of the Pharaohs trouble me still." We continued to discuss these things for some hours.

Paul was mostly quiet. I remember not how the conversation turned, but at a certain point he asked, "What do the followers of the Christus believe about these things?"

At that time I was ignorant and replied, "They do not honor the gods at all, are accused of consuming their own young, and of all sorts of abominable things."

It was Fulvia who laughed at this. "I have a dear friend Benedicta. She is a noble woman, and I can assure you that she does not eat her young. She belongs to this new Way. She does worship, but not like most others. I will bring her here so we can continue this discussion."

Paul added, "Our Emperor also honors this new Way. He would not do so if such things were true, it would seem. What do you think, John?" I shrugged. With that we concluded our conversation, but opened a new path without realizing it

\*\*\*

That very next week, Fulvia brought the noble woman named Benedicta. She was a beautiful lady who had completed the time of childbirth, and was married to a patrician who was a leader in the city. She was dressed simply, yet elegantly, and had her hair in the style that Roman patrician women prefer. As she entered, she greeted Paul and me, and we led her in for some refreshment. To my surprise, when Gallicanus came bringing the drink, she rose from her place and embraced him as an equal, and he received the embrace without shame. Seeing my surprise, Benedicta said, "Did you not know that your Gallicanus is a follower of the Christus also?" Though Gallicanus had worked for us now for some time, I had not known this, and grew even more intrigued. I had never seen a noble woman treat a slave as her equal, and Paul was especially eager to understand this thing that united them.

When I think back on that evening, I am amazed by the patience of both Benedicta and Gallicanus as they tried to explain their belief to Fulvia, Paul, and me. I do not recall their exact words, but I do remember what we understood. We imagined this god who they described as something like Apollo, who had descended onto earth to dwell with men. These men became his enemy, and then put the god to death, but a few honored him and still honor him today, for what reason, none of us could fathom!

"Is this not the meaning of what you have told us?" Paul inquired, after they had been speaking to us of these matters for hours.

"Yes and no," Benedicta said, as she glanced over at Gallicanus. There was a long silence.

Finally, Gallicanus proposed, "Let me bring you to see. It is easier to see than to explain."

\*\*\*

Benedicta could not accompany us on our excursion some days later, but Gallicanus led us across the city to a hill on the other side of the Tiber, where there was a cemetery which neither of us was happy about entering. "Come," Gallicanus prodded us, and we approached a small shrine with red walls and two small pillars. There were many flowers and offerings around this tomb.

"Why do so many come to this spot to honor this dead man?" Paul inquired.

"Because this is where Peter is buried," Gallicanus replied. He motioned that we sit on some stones, and he continued. "Let me tell you about him. Rome was his city, and the followers of the new Way loved him, as he loved them. He died near this spot, killed by those who tried to stop the new Way from spreading. We love him still, for he was so like us. He was human, he was weak, he was fearful, and he did not want to die." Paul interrupted "So why did he not flee, or ask those who loved him to free him?"

Gallicanus paused and replied, "He could have escaped, and even began to flee Rome. Then he stopped and realized that he loved this Christus, loved him more than life itself. So he returned, and gave his life."

I was perplexed as was Paul. "*Love* a god? I understand *honoring*, respecting, even fearing, but *loving* a god? It doesn't make any sense," I objected.

Gallicanus looked at me and said, "Would you not place yourself in danger if you were in battle, in order to save Paul? Would not Paul do the same? Why?" He paused, then continued, "It is the same here. If the Christus is as real as Paul, why can one not love him? This is why we honor Peter, because of his love." Interiorly, I scoffed at his words. Paul, however, seemed intrigued.

The following week Benedicta offered to show us other examples of the Way she followed, so we arrived at one of the *diakonias*[30] within the city of Rome. These were places where some devoted themselves to caring for the poor, orphans, and widows.

"Is this not a work to be carried out by the magistrates, because these Romans are not to be neglected by those in the Senate?" Paul asked.

Benedicta responded, "If Fulvia were hungry, would you have her wait for a magistrate to help her, or would you not immediately give her to eat? If John was without a place to sleep, would you not offer him lodging, or would you advise him to seek out a senator? Here it is not a matter of what *should* be done, but what *I* can do for those who are my brothers and sisters. Following the Christus makes us all one."

---

[30] The *diakonia* was a place administered by the early Christian communities in Rome where those in need could obtain assistance.

Paul inquired, "What do you do for those in need?"

She replied, "I give all my husband will permit to this *diakonia*, so that food and lodgings may be available. It is never enough." She paused as we watched the activities of those distributing the food. Then she continued, "But what is important is not how much one does, but why one does it." We continued to walk, observing the activity and several women resting from the hot sun under the balcony, eating what they had been given.

"Why do you do this, Benedicta?" I asked.

She let a long time go by before she responded, "Love."

"That word again!" Paul broke in as he threw up his arm.

Benedicta, always good-willed, smiled. "Perhaps that is enough for today. Would you walk me toward my home?" she asked, and we accepted.

As we made our way back toward our homes, passing by *insulae* and vendors, I noticed many people who lacked what they needed. Because Rome was full of these people, I had never paid much attention to them.

As we prepared to go our separate ways, Benedicta stopped us and asked, "What do you do for those in need?"

Before I could even think, Paul responded, "I do nothing." Then we walked home in silence.

A week passed, and seeing that the tomb of Peter and the *diakonia* started to stir Paul up, I became uneasy. I therefore asked him, "Should we discontinue this inquiry? After all, we have our gods, and Mithras has been good to us."

He reflected and replied, "I do not think we should run as if faced with an enemy. In fact, we have never fled from an adversary or any other in our lives. Let us inquire further to see what this new Way is."

I objected, "But how can we discover anything, because this Christus in whom they place their trust is no longer alive?"

Paul irritated me when he replied, "Those who follow him claim he is still alive, and is the reason they are one. Let us seek the truth of this." I was more hesitant to search this out than Paul, but for now at least, I resolved to investigate further, mostly out of deference to him.

Benedicta became our principal guide, with Gallicanus sometimes accompanying us. They brought us to a meeting of the leaders of the *diakonia* in the city, during which ways to help those in need were discussed. This is how we met Cornelius, Maximus, and Gallus, who greeted us graciously because Benedicta introduced us as her friends. We spent the afternoon together and ended up speaking, not of their beliefs in this new god, but rather about Paul and me, for they were quite interested in our lives up to this point. I was more reserved, but Paul shared with them facts from his difficult childhood, his time in the legion in Germania, his meeting with me, and our adventure in bringing Constantina to Rome. These men, or "elders," were kind and gentle, and seemed to have no desire to convince us of the truth of their god. They showed an interest in our lives, and a willingness to share theirs with us within a friendship. Paul greeted this with trust, but I, with suspicion.

It was night by the time we left their company and made our way across the city. Paul seemed content. I asked him, "What do you think of Benedicta and Gallicanus, and these men we have just met, Paul?"

We stopped and he reflected for a moment. He then turned and looked at me. "I am struck by the way that they seem to rejoice in one another. Could it be that this Christus is present there, and that is how he is loved?" I said nothing, and we continued to make our way home.

I thought for a long while of Paul's words that night, and every time I thought of them I grew angry. Were not Mithras and the other gods enough? Had our gods not protected us in battle, rescued Paul from a miserable life, brought me back from Egypt, graced us with our home and present status? This was sufficient for me. Why was it not for Paul? I wondered about this. I felt a space, like a fog, growing between us, which I had never sensed before. But I spoke not a word of this to him.

*\*\*\**

It was our custom to maintain our skill at battle by sparring with each other, and we did this several times a week at the garrison near our home. This had been our practice since we had met each other in Germania. Several weeks after meeting with the elders, Paul and I were so engaged but I became angry, and then enraged, at him. The sparring became an emotional battle in which I truly tried to do him harm. Paul's smile turned to a frown when I became aggressive with my sword, and he had to defend himself with the skill he had acquired in the field. He was an expert soldier, and after several minutes of fighting, as my rage grew, he was able to knock my sword out of my hand and pointed his at me. "What is it, brother?" he asked. I simply looked at him, threw my helmet down, and walked away.

I was furious, and I avoided Paul for some time. When I saw him the next day and he inquired again as to why I was so inclined to anger toward him, I refused to answer. I remained in this state for several months, seeing the one I had beheld as my dearest friend in the past, as a traitor in the present. I continued to approach Mithras with sacrifice and attend to him at the Mithraeum across the city. At this point, Paul probably would have accompanied me, but I did not ask him, and held his absence against him also. As I sat in the dark Mithreaum, gazing at the figure of the god, I resolved to always be faithful to the one who had brought me out of Egypt to this place. I asked Mithras not to punish Paul too severely for his dishonor.

As I walked home after this visit, I stopped and looked at those places that had once given me peace, especially a vantage point that overlooked the Tiber, to which I would often walk with Paul in the past. I no longer had peace; I was angry with him for being drawn toward the new Way, and I was angry with myself for harboring such feelings against one who had done nothing against me. I saw no way to dispel my anger. My heart was a cage; I was imprisoned.

In this state, I made my way to the house of Fulvia. "I have noted that you are sad, and Paul has inquired of me what he might do to ease your pain. But because no one knows its cause, no one can help you bear it," she said, as I sat with her. I revealed to her my growing feeling of betrayal by Paul. I explained that, as he became more interested in the new Way, and seemed to want to believe in their Christus, he was abandoning Mithras who had always been good and faithful. "Can he not honor both?" she asked. I explained to her what Benedicta had told us: that followers of the new Way hold that all gods are false but Christus. I expected my sister to be shocked at this notion, but she seemed not perturbed at all. "Is this new Way helping Paul? Is he more content, or at peace?" she inquired.

"What is your meaning?" I asked, perplexed.

She turned toward me and looked me in the eyes. "If I found a god, or a friend, or a new shop, or a new home that made my life easier, that made me more content, I would expect those who have affection for me to rejoice, and not to hold it against me. At least I would expect this if their affection were true." With these words she kissed me, and left me sitting in her garden. Later, as I walked through the streets of Rome, avoiding that road which would lead to my home, her words began to burn in my heart.

From that day onward, I resolved to observe Paul more closely, so that I might see what changes this new Way might bring to him. He had always been restless, looking for that next great adventure, ready to ride off for a battle, or a fight, or the races. Over the next days and weeks, I did notice that he seemed to be more at ease, desiring less to chase after whatever excitement he could find. This was the first change, though slight, that I saw. Besides this, there was something else that was different. Neither Paul, nor I for that matter, had ever paid attention to strangers in need. Paul had always been generous with his men and comrades, but never toward a stranger. After all, what did the unknown have to do with him? I saw that he began to notice those in misery in the streets of Rome. I saw him give money to some, and others he looked at with pain on his face. This was not the Paul I knew in Germania. Something was changing here.

During this entire period, which must have been difficult for him because we shared the same dwelling, and I had been so irritated, he never challenged me on how I felt, or tried to convince me to follow this Way with him. But I could see that he was concerned, for Paul had always been protective, and my sadness certainly weighed on him. But I did not know how to console his or my heart, so I did not attempt to do so. I only continued to observe him, and slowly, in this way, my anger began to subside.

It was after months of sadness that I finally approached Paul. "Can I speak with you in the garden?" I asked, and we made our way to that place of springtime and hope that my sister had created.

"I have been angry and bitter toward you, and for this I have been also angry at myself. I saw you as one who has betrayed the gods and what they have given us, and I saw you walking a path different from the one I am on. This also filled me with indignation, for I realized that I could not walk that Way with you. It seemed to me that you had abandoned both the gods and those that hold you in their heart. I was furious. But then I realized that my anger was indeed selfish, that I sought not even to see if this path was a better way for you. Resentment blinded me, and I am sorry. I want to say that if you wish to walk this Way, I will not oppose you…"

At this point Paul interrupted me by putting his hand on my shoulder and said, "It has indeed sorrowed me to see you in this state, John. I have felt your sadness and carried it within me all these months. I hope we can find the way to greater contentment now." He smiled and we both rose and began to walk down the hill on which our home was situated.

"Can I explain to you, John, this path, as I see it? That way you can understand why it is drawing me, and we will not be divided. Perhaps this new Way is not a betrayal to Mithras. Perhaps, indeed, it is our very devotion to this god which has led us to this point. Perhaps even, my brother, I…we… are not breaking off from that faith at all, but are merely continuing on it in a new and truer way. Could not Mithras himself be a shadow of this Christus? Why could it not be thus? I know not the answer yet, but will you not see if this is so with me, John? Will you walk this path with me, to see where it leads? If it leads to falsehood, indeed we must save each other from it. But perhaps it leads not away from, but rather toward something. Let us see together." We stopped at the bottom of the hill.

I had lost that deadness of heart that had shielded me in the land of the Pharaohs, and by the time Paul had completed these words, tears were streaming down my face. Being a soldier, I turned, so as not to be shamed.

I faced him once more and I was relieved, as if a great weight had been lifted which I was no longer able to carry. His words consoled my heart, for I was not condemned for my hesitation, but rather invited to this road while carrying all of my misgivings. The invitation to verify whether this Way were true was not threatening to me; it would be one more journey added to the others that Paul and I had taken in the past. I accepted, having no idea of how my life would be transformed.

# Chapter 8: The Way

"These should be placed in front so that we will use them first," Paul said to Gallicanus. We were together on the subterranean level of our home, where Gallicanus had been acquiring and storing various wines and oils, arranged according to type and quality.

"Yes master. And the newer wines?" This was a work that gave Gallicanus much satisfaction, and we were also pleased. We continued to discuss the arrangement and what still needed to be acquired. "I will take care of the ordering and placement of all that we need, master."

Before leaving for the upper level, Paul turned and asked him to sit for a moment. "Gallicanus, may I ask why you follow this Way?"

He instantly responded, "Because it is the place where I am embraced, it is a place of hope, and it is on this Way that I find the Christus alive."

"But," I interjected, "What makes the followers of this Way different from, say, Paul, or Fulvia, or me, or any other you can point out?"

Gallicanus seemed a bit embarrassed by my question. After a pause he said, "I judge not what is in the heart of others, and I judge not you, my masters. On the contrary, I hold you in great esteem. If you ask me what I see in those who follow the Way, I can only say that I have never seen such compassion in those who have possessions, and such gratitude in those who have nothing. I have asked myself again and again, 'What makes these people content, even in adversity?' They are as one, like the members of a body, each one caring for the other. In their love for one another they find the Christus still alive. And when I follow this Way, I am able to taste just a bit of this, like this wine," he said, holding up an amphora. He continued, "This wine is the finest you have. Just a taste of this, and you will not be satisfied with any of the rest. It is the same reason why I follow."

That day we began to see Gallicanus, not as a slave, but as a friend. We esteemed him greatly, as we were actually learning about the Way through him. This was the first change in our daily lives.

The second change that took place was a few months after this. Crispus and Crispinianus received orders to return from the north to Ostia, where they would be stationed permanently. When we saw them, Paul spoke of our attempt to verify the claim of those who followed the Christus. Crispus was the first to call the Way "Paul's Quest" (*Quaesitus Paulis*), and Paul became nicknamed "Odysseus" from that moment, for his spirit was leading us on this search. We all laughed. Looking back now, it did seem an adventure to us, and Crispus and Crispinianus were indeed eager to join in, as if we had invited them to a battle practice.

Benedicta came to our house on occasion because we had become friends. Being of noble birth, she reminded me of Constantina, in that her human qualities overshadowed her patrician background. She seemed to enjoy our company, and she was a welcome guest, even when not accompanied by Fulvia. She was at our home one day when Crispus and Crispinianus were present, and as Gallicanus served, I made a request. "Please take us to your place of worship, so we can observe how you honor the Christus."

I noticed that she and Gallicanus looked at one another and

seemed embarrassed. When she was silent, Gallicanus rescued her by saying, "I am sorry, masters, but she cannot. Only the initiated may participate in the breaking of the bread."[31]

I was perplexed and asked, "But why? What is there to hide?"

Benedicta replied, "Just as the intimate moments of a family are not for strangers to share, it is the same with these mysteries. The Christus is present in the breaking of the bread in a way that only the initiated can partake of. There is nothing to hide. I can tell you what takes place: the elder comes and says the blessing and breaks the bread, and all partake of the body and blood of the Christus. It is so celebrated, as we were commanded to do. Then there is a feast, an *Agape*[32], in which food is brought and shared by all, without distinction. Then we greet one another and go home. That is all."

I broke in, "It almost sounds like the rites of Mithras, except the blood of the bull is replaced by that of Christus. But how do you obtain his blood? Is it smeared upon your head, as Mithras requires?"

Benedicta looked perplexed, and looked to Gallicanus for aid. He broke in. "Masters, it is a similar thing in some ways, for it is by blood that one is purified. But in our rites you do not see blood; you see only bread and wine. You only see blood with your other eyes, eyes of belief. It is difficult to make clear. Perhaps," he began as he looked at Benedicta, "I will introduce you to someone who can explain things better than I," and he and Benedicta nodded at each other. I did not understand what he was saying at the time: blood, sacrifice, bread, *agape*. I knew it was important for them to meet together and to hold these rites, and they seemed to rejoice in anticipation of this meeting. But their explanation only made me more confused.

---

[31] *Didache*, 9.5

[32] The *Agape* was a "love feast" in which food was shared and friendship celebrated. This followed the breaking of the bread. Tertullian, *Apology*, 39.16.

My resistance was breaking down without my realizing it, as the four of us, all soldiers, found ourselves drawn into the lives of the followers of the new Way. Fulvia, due to her duties with her household, was rarely able to participate. Soon we were regular participants both helping the *diakonia* as well as spending time with these new friends. We offered our dwelling as a place where the leaders could meet, and soon our home was filled with that rejoicing in one another that we found so attractive.

As the weeks and months passed, it was as if a silent desire began to grow to belong more completely to this Way of life. Paul was the first to express it, "I too want to follow this Christus, but let us seek out the elders and speak with them." Crispus saluted him as Odysseus, expressing our acceptance of the next step.

It was Benedicta who had introduced us to the elders Cornelius and Gallus, who had age and wisdom as well as faith in the Christus. They embraced us warmly one evening in a humble home. "What rules must one adhere to in order to belong to Christus and to his followers?" Paul asked.

Cornelius squinted and said "Rules? Who told you there were rules you must abide by before you can follow this Way?"

I responded, "Every god has requirements of those who honor him. Is it not the same with the Christus? Gallicanus, for example, said that one must forgive one's enemy. Now for a soldier, that is impossible because…"

Cornelius interrupted me and said, "I don't want you to worry about that for now. For you, the only recommendation, not rule, I have is to remain with us. There you will discover Christus and he will transform your heart. Worry not about the rest."

Paul was reflecting and asked, "What about loving another? Is that permitted in the new Way?"

Cornelius looked with compassion on Paul, then at me. "He takes all human love and transforms it into something greater.

Instead of renouncing love, your capacity for it will grow. In him, your love for one another will blossom forth and embrace others also, especially those in need. But you do not need my words to tell you this, for you have seen it. You will continue to see it." Crispus and Crispinianus had been silent. "And what about these friends? You are always welcome here. Are you still in the legion?" Cornelius asked. And hence a long conversation began among the three of them, not about the Way, but about their lives as soldiers.

"I like this Cornelius," Crispus said upon leaving.

As we walked home, before returning to the garrison, Crispinianus said to Paul, "Odysseus, our adventure continues. I am on the voyage with you until the end!" We parted ways for the night.

The quest we embarked on did indeed continue, and my sense of resistance became a memory. I still had questions, and poor Gallicanus had to hear and attempt to respond to all of them. It was still unclear to me why one could not honor both Mithras and the Christus, as it was equally unclear what made this new Way different from other paths. He must have become exasperated with me, for one day he approached me and said, "I have spoken with Benedicta, and she has arranged a meeting for you with Theophanes, a Greek follower of the Way, a great and learned man from Alexandria. He may be able to answer all your questions that I cannot." I accepted the invitation and asked Paul to accompany me.

***

Theophanes was in Rome on some business of his own, and we met him at an inn on the outskirts of the city. He was an older man, with a white beard and hair, but had the bearing of one younger in years. His eyes were those of one who had studied much of the wisdom of the past. He greeted us warmly and invited us to walk with him to a quiet spot under the trees. It was good to be outside the city. The serenity of this place calmed my burning questions. "I have heard that you have begun to inquire whether following the Christus is a path that you might walk." He paused and looked at us. "I am not going to convince you of such, my friends, for this is the task for your heart. I will not give you cunning arguments, or even answer all of your questions, in order to seduce you to follow this Way. No. With this clear, now we can enjoy these calm moments together." And with these words, he was silent. Paul and I were surprised, and did not know what to say. "Have you been to Alexandria?" Theophanes asked.

"Yes," I began, and told him of my three years there, and I asked if he knew that inn where I had met Merytre. Unfortunately, he did not. We sat under the trees as a slight breeze rustled the pines above. It was a beautiful day.

After a while, Theophanes turned to me. "When you were in Alexandria, John, what did you desire most?"

I thought a moment and replied, "To be with those who I have most affection for."

Theophanes nodded and said, "Ah, love, yes." Some time passed before he asked again, "And you, Paul, when John was sent unjustly away, what did you wish for most?"

Paul responded, "The same. That John would be able to join us here."

Theophanes thought a moment and said, "Yes, to be united with those one loves, to be one. Pardon me if I continue with these questions, but this is how I learn. What is it that you love most in another person?"

Paul and I thought for a long time, for this was a difficult question. Paul answered, "What I love most is what is good in them, that goodness that I am able to see more clearly than others are able."

Theophanes' eyes lit up and he responded, "Ah yes, goodness, what is good. To be united with what is good." After a while he continued, "And what has made you most sad, or angry, or both, in your relations to others?"

I immediately thought of Terentianus as I said, "When an untruth is said of another."

Theophanes again nodded and said, "So love of truth, hatred of untruth. Yes...." We all sat there and contemplated these words. It was a long time before any of us spoke again.

"What I have understood from you," Theophanes began, "is that what you, as men, desire most is to embrace what is true, and this we call justice, to be united with what is good, which we call love. These are among our greatest desires, beyond eating and propagating. These greatest desires, this heart if you will, sends us on a journey to gather clues. Clues to what? What is it, my friends, that can fill this longing for what is true? What is so great that, once it is found, you need not seek more? What is the greatest good? What is beauty itself, and not merely its reflection? Look over there." He motioned toward the hills, which were hazy blue, and the sky, which was as orange as the sun was, disappearing over the horizon. "You are drawn to what is beautiful, to what is good and true. You have told me so with your own words. I have learned much from you this day," he said, with a smile. He turned and continued to gaze at the setting sun.

He turned to Paul and said, "It was Plato himself who said that we seek a beautiful man or woman, only to find that their beauty is incomplete. We then seek another, and another, until we realize that what we are grasping at is beauty itself. Or we cling to a person, or even a thing, thinking that this, finally, will fill our being with happiness, only to find it too is incomplete. So we seek another, and then others, until some men discover that it is happiness itself that we seek, not those things in which happiness dwells only partially. It is the same with truth; the more one pursues it, the more it flees. Yes, the things of this world are but signs along the way, leading to that one Being which, in itself, just is, and not because of another. That Being which contains the fullness, from which all else derives. These are your words, these are the words of the philosopher. You have indicated your own path."

"I would not tell you to follow this Way," he began again after a pause, "if it would mean repressing the desires of which we have spoken. If you ignore your own heart, there would be no difference between this Way and following the many gods that you Romans are fond of adopting. No, do not follow the Christus if this means that you retreat from yourself. I would ask you to pay more attention to your own heart, for it is your heart which is the place where those great desires, those longings which make you a man, are lodged. The greatest philosophers were aware of that part of themselves of which we are speaking. What is new about this Way is its claim, for it is only this god, this Christus, who claims to be the only one who can fill that heart of which you are made, my friends. Verify if this Way can indeed answer that heart; if it cannot, abandon it and search further. But if it can, then you have found a happiness and peace which none can take from you. It is indeed a journey, a journey to be aware of who you are. For if your life is not a question, then the Christus is not an answer."

After a while I asked, "But how do we do this, Theophanes?"

He seemed surprised, and responded, "Oh, verify what you have seen. See if this Way makes you greater than what you have been. See if it gives you greater joy. Does it enlarge the thirst you have for life? Does it enlarge your capacity to welcome others? Does it give you greater hope? Do you find something more true? A greater love? This is the only proof that can be given whether this path is for you. Be true to yourselves as you verify the truth of this claim, and you will not be led astray."

This was not the way I had expected Theophanes to deal with the uncertainties that I had brought. My comparisons with following the Mithraic way and that of the Christus faded, as I strove to understand what he had laid before us. "Follow the way indicated by your heart; there you will find the clues that will lead you on your journey." This is how I then understood his words, and I sought to uncover those desires which have no limit.

The next time we saw Crispus and Crispinianus, we tried to explain to them our meeting with Theophanes, but we made them, and ourselves, more confused than before. "Odysseus," Crispus addressed Paul, "let us continue to live the life of those who follow the Christus. Only so may we see if it is a truer way for us."

Paul's eyes grew wide as he turned to me and said, "I believe this is what Theophanes was trying to tell us." It was agreed.

We continued to fulfill our duties, to help at the *diakonia*, and to stay with those friends already on this Way. We did this without any plans or expectations. Though Crispus and Crispinianus had less time than Paul and I, because they were still in the legion, they accompanied us whenever their duties would permit. Our friendship with them grew immensely.

\*\*\*

"What an adventure every day has become, without having to travel from the place where we live!" Paul exclaimed one evening when Crispus, Crispinianus, Paul, and I were together. It was indeed a path toward a destiny which drew us and embraced us; it seemed as if the events that had happened before had led to this point. I no longer felt I was betraying Mithras or my following of him; the one was simply a prelude to the other. This only became clear to me through the experience of following the Christus, and of belonging to this community, not through a convincing explanation at all. When we spoke about requesting to be initiated into the new Way, it seemed the natural next step, not as if we were breaking away or betraying anything or anyone.

When I told Fulvia of my decision to be initiated, she seemed troubled. "Have you not been happy until now? Why would you change your life so drastically? Has another influenced you?" and she continued with such questions.

"Dear sister, of course I have been happy; you can see that. And I love my life here, and I love my friends who are my family. I do not know how to explain this, except to say that it is something beautiful that I want to partake of. It is a more joyful way of living which I want to follow and learn. Remember your words to me when I did not understand the actions of Paul. It is the same here. Be not upset, dear sister." I approached her and kissed her on her head, and embraced her. Then I bent down, for she was shorter than I, and said, slowly, "You will not lose me Fulvia. I will always love you, and my love will not diminish. I will love you even more than I have in the past. This is not a separation which will divide us, but will unite us, whether you choose to follow the new Way or not. Trust me, sister." With these words she was calmed. I was calmed also, because I knew that my sister relied on my strength and affection, notwithstanding the fact that she had her own children and husband. It was as if she needed my love to feel stable, even within her own family. But because I loved her dearly, I would always offer her my heart and all that I had.

*** 

When the time came for our initiation, I was no longer plagued by doubts or feelings of betrayal of the gods that had come before. I did not understand everything about the Way, or about the things that the Christus had taught. But it was not a matter of my understanding or agreeing with a set of precepts. This was a life that had embraced me, and the understanding would come along in time. I did indeed follow the advice of Theophanes, and realized that my heart was fuller than before, and the others who followed the Way were not extraneous to my own person. The feeling of belonging overwhelmed me.

Besides Paul, Crispus, Crispinianus, and I, there were nearly twenty others initiated that day. Seven or so were from the legion, and the rest ranged from patricians to the destitute. These were my people now, and I was theirs. At the *Agape* that followed, I looked around and marveled at the manner in which the people treated one another as one, without distinction of class or wealth. It was something extraordinary. These were my thoughts when Benedicta and Gallicanus came to greet and embrace us. I turned to Paul to speak to him, but I noticed that he seemed deeply moved. He had been quiet for quite some time, which was not like him, and his eyes were moist, which was also not like him. As Crispus and Crispinianus chatted away, I let Paul rest in those feelings which were embracing his soul at that moment.

The next day, among other things, we discussed Gallicanus; it did not seem right that he who had led us along this path be kept in an inferior position. We made our decision and called him in. "We are offering you your freedom, Gallicanus," I explained.

"But master," he replied, "I have no funds to purchase my freedom."

Paul broke in. "Gallicanus, you do not owe us anything. We want to make you a free man because we want to do so, and we do not need money for this. If you choose to remain in our employment we will pay you wages, and you can still dwell here, if you wish." Gallicanus smiled as he accepted. It took many months for him to stop calling us "master."

# Chapter 9: The Garden

My sister had not been part of the most recent events, and it was perhaps because she feared to be left out that she came to see me some days after the initiation. I was sure the new Way would not lead me away from Fulvia, but she seemed to need constant reassurance of this. She brought her oldest son, Pachamius, who was eager to help Gallicanus go to the market. Gallicanus showed her in while I completed some tasks in another part of our home.

\*\*\*

Fulvia was waiting for me in the garden in front of the *nymphaeum*[33] which she had designed. As I approached her, sitting among the flowers and shafts of sunlight, she seemed lost in thought. "Sister, why so serious on such a glorious day in our little patch of paradise?" Fulvia's visits always pleased me.

"Brother!" she said, as she embraced me. Over the years, Fulvia and I had no need to speak many words in order to communicate. We both sat and listened to the water flow over the rocks and down into the lower levels of the fountain. We could hear faint voices coming from the outside world. Her hands were so small in mine that, as we sat, I seemed to be

---

[33] A Roman shrine and fountain, usually dedicated to a nymph.

holding those of a child.

I knew something was on my sister's mind, but I let her express it when she was ready. "John, when will you marry? I already have four children. You have a home and the means to do as I have done. Why do you wait?" She had said these words before on several occasions, but never with this insistence.

"Why do you bring this up now, my sister?" I said with some impatience. Then I looked upon her and saw the concern on her face. I knew she had my interests at heart, so I replied, "Sister, do you want me to be happy?"

"Of course, brother. That is why I ask you these things. I want this for you most of all."

I motioned in the direction of Paul, who was still inside the house.

"I am happy. If I am happy, why should I change?"

"You lack nothing, then?" she asked. I looked at her so that I could understand the full meaning of her words. She had tears in her eyes. I reached out and turned her face toward mine. "Nothing, dear sister," and I kissed her on the forehead.

We sat next to each other as the water from the fountains poured into the basins below. Paul entered and kissed Fulvia as he sat beside me. Perhaps this is what happiness is, I thought. If I could prolong this moment and live it over and over again, with the ones that I love the most, this would be enough.

As he motioned towards the figures above the fountain, Paul chuckled, "Behold the divine family!" We looked at Fulvia as Persephone, our mother on her right as Demeter, and I as Bacchus.[34] I squeezed my sister's hand.

After a time Fulvia turned and gazed at both of us. I believe

---

[34] Demeter was the goddess of the harvest. Her one daughter Persephone was taken by Hades to the underworld, where she would reside for one third of the year, thus explaining the bareness of winter as Demeter mourned the absence of her daughter. This myth was very popular in this era because it dealt with the questions of loss and death. Bacchus was the god of wine, representing both the celebration of life and its pitfalls.

she understood the meaning behind my words.

There was noise again in the house as Gallicanus and Pachamius returned. "Will you stay for dinner?" Gallicanus asked Fulvia.

She laughed and said, "If I do, I fear my husband will marry another from desperation. I cannot. But I will next week, I promise." We then began speaking of various people and events until we arrived at a subject that I was sure she was pining to address.

"How was the initiation? What did they do? Is it so secret that you cannot tell?" I chuckled, and told her of the entire rite. "Is that all? Why all that fuss, and stories of blood? I never believed any of them, but why tell such things if the initiation is so simple?" I did not know how to answer her inquiry, because I did not understand either, why such things were said of the followers of the Way.

She stood and I asked, "Must you go already?" She sat back down beside us. I took her hand, and the three of us sat there again for a long time, enjoying the coolness of the water as it flowed down, and the soft breeze that rustled the leaves of the plants Fulvia had placed in that spot.

\*\*\*

In one way, nothing changed, and in another way, everything. As that first year after our initiation turned into the next, we still did many things we had done before. Paul, Crispus, Crispinianus, and I went to the races whenever we could find the time. Paul kept his irascible character, and I still felt myself a legionary at heart. Yet everything was different. Though we maintained previous friendships, we made new relations with those with whom, if it were not for the new Way, we would have had no contact or interest whatsoever. I too began to notice those in need, even if they were not of my family or friends. It now seemed that even these were somehow part of my life, in a way I could not yet understand, but could not ignore. Paul and I, as well as Crispus and Crispinianus when they were in Rome, aided the *diakonia* several times a week.

Gallicanus remained in our service, though he obtained his own dwelling the third year after his release. He also remained our companion and friend.

Crispus and Crispinianus took their commitment to the new Way seriously. They lived in Ostia and were always at each other's side. They often brought people to our home, especially from the garrisons, who wanted to know about the Way. Our dwelling became a place of new encounters, affection, and excitement.

These were indeed happy times. It was easy to be grateful in those days, for our sufferings were few.

# Chapter 10: Imperial Changes

It seemed like it was only months after these events, but it was indeed years, when word reached us of the sudden death of our beloved Emperor Constantine.[35] He was in the midst of planning a campaign against the Persian aggression in the east. We had seldom seen him in Rome, but his death saddened all of us, and we wondered, as all Romans did, what changes would now take place.

The three sons who bore his name battled for control of the Empire, but much of their disagreement and fighting was taking place outside of Rome. We heard of rivals in Constantine's line being murdered or disappearing, of armies being raised, of battles being fought. Finally the Empire was divided between our glorious Emperor's three sons Constantine II, Constantius II and Constans. Years went by in which there was no unity in the Empire, and no one seemed to understand who was in control. Buildings and roads disintegrated, and farms were abandoned as more of the poor came to the cities to seek employment and food. This influx of the needy caused a crisis in Rome, which no one was able or cared to take on, because battles for power were occupying the attention of those who were supposed to care for the people. Though it was upsetting to see our city and the Empire so neglected, we tried to continue our life and work as

---

[35] Emperor Constantine died in 337 C.E.

before. The need at the *diakonia* was greater than our ability, and we all found ourselves working harder to help those we could.

Through a series of deaths and battles, which few seemed to understand, the nephew of Constantine, Julian, came to power, and was proclaimed Caesar by the armies of the north.[36] At the time, this seemed of no importance to us, because word got around that this new Emperor would remain with his troops in order to push back the Germanic tribes, a task that Paul knew would keep the Emperor away from Rome. Hence, Julian was far from our thought, until one day a series of new decrees were read in the Forum.

\*\*\*

It was odd how what is good at one moment is considered evil at another. Before Constantine, it was honorable to worship the ancient gods, and evil to worship the Christus. Our great Emperor made the latter legal, and tolerated the worship of the former. When Julian came to power, things had gone back to before: the new Way was evil, the old gods were good.

With the reign of Julian, the situation in the Empire grew worse. The lack of leadership caused great poverty and misfortune. Everything was falling apart. Even the entertainment at the Circus ceased, so impoverished the city of the Caesars became. It was said that the borders which we had worked so hard to guard were now open to whatever barbarian tribe wished to enter. Every day, as we walked the streets, one could hear Romans arguing, trying to place the blame. I found myself arguing that what is lacking is a man who can lead the whole Empire, as Constantine had done.

It is easier to blame others rather than oneself, and perhaps this is why the new Emperor, Julian, stated that the reason that the Empire was in disarray was that the gods of old were no

---

[36] Julian, known as the Apostate, reigned from 360 until June 26, 363 C.E.

longer being honored. He claimed that Rome had lost its soul and that the "Galileans," as he called the followers of the Way, were responsible for this. For this reason, he began to pass decrees in order to lessen the influence of followers of the Christus. At first he only restricted the freedom of schools, and took away properties that Constantine had set aside for the use of the followers of the Way.[37] These were minor, but his decrees became increasingly harsh, to the point that our community began to feel threatened.

Soon after the new laws were passed, work began to repair some of the temples to the ancient gods, and men were recruited to serve as priests to perform the rites. This was an oddity even for those who were not followers of the Way, including my sister Fulvia. She continued to honor our ancestors, but practiced neither ancient nor new public rites. "They're only serving as priests because it means free food and lodging," she commented, as we passed a procession heading toward the temple of Jupiter. The strange thing was that the Emperor was trying to revive the ancient religions with decrees, but the people were completely indifferent. There were priests frequenting the temples because they were employed to do so, but many Romans I observed expressed that the buildings would be better used for shops and businesses, as most had become before the decrees were implemented.

Neither Paul nor I, nor any of our friends, intended to be caught up in these laws by challenging them, but neither did we intend to deny our following of the new Way. Over the past years we had seen many political changes in Rome, and we thought that these new waves would leave us untouched, as they had for so long. After all, there were so few public worshipers of the ancient gods. Why would the Emperor be concerned about those who followed the Christus?

Our complacency lasted only two months, until word reached

---

[37] *Ecclesiastical History*, Socrates Scholasticus, 3.11 and 12.

Rome that the Emperor was indeed enforcing his policies, and that men and women who refused his orders to worship the gods of old were being put to death. When he published his work *Against the Galileans*[38], we could feel the fear sweep through the followers of the Way, like leaves fluttering in a new wind. There was much talk of how one could follow the Christus and escape punishment at the same time. To me, it still all seemed distant, for those who had been punished or executed for disobedience were far from Rome, as was Julian himself. Some of our friends, however, grew more alarmed. Paul and I continued our lives unchanged.

\*\*\*

During this tumultuous period, Paul and I met a Commander whose name was also Gallicanus, like our former slave. He was stationed in Rome at the time and, notwithstanding the state of affairs, had expressed interest in the new Way. "Do you think he might be a spy?" Crispus asked me the day after we had met.

"No," Paul replied. "I am certain of it." Paul had a sense for the character of others, and he based his judgment on this. I could see that Crispus was still uncertain.

"We have invited him to spend time with us so we can get to know him, and he can know the Way. We will not put anyone in danger," I reassured him.

Over the next days and weeks, I remained impressed by Gallicanus. Because he had been Consul some years earlier, his interest in the Christus put him at some risk, yet he persisted. We had many similarities, both in our background in the legion and in the questions he brought to us. "I have been devoted to Mithras since my first years serving Rome," he began one day.

At that, Paul said, "Then you and John must talk," at which point I engaged Commander Gallicanus in a lengthy discussion

---

[38] *Against the Galileans* was published in 361 C.E.

on how many see Mithras as a figure of the Christus.

"Just as Mithras slew the bull in obedience to the Sun, and from its blood all life sprang, so the Christus obeyed the will of his Father, and from his blood this new life comes forth," I explained. But these were just words; Gallicanus needed to see the life which springs from the sacrifice of the Christus.

As others had done for us, we brought the Commander to those people and places where the new Way was most manifest. Because he was stationed in Rome, he would also often come to our home, which had become a center of activity for the *diakonia*, the breaking of the bread, and many other encounters. Eventually, he too asked to be initiated, and asked Paul and me to accompany him on this path. We accepted with gratitude.

It was only later that the Commander's initiation caused a stir, for the Emperor was attempting to diminish the number of followers of the Way. Instead they were increasing. In the eyes of certain magistrates, Paul and I were "blamed" for leading Commander Gallicanus to the Christus. Without realizing it at the time, we began to be under the scrutiny of those who held power in the city.

# Chapter 11: Destiny Beckons

I remember that it was on a warm evening when we were gathered together, Paul, Crispus, Crispinianus, Benedicta, and I. Crispus began, "We cannot follow the Way as openly as before. The laws forbid it. The Emperor will not tolerate those who go against his policies. Both of you, John and Paul, must be especially careful. You are both so well known, your home such a center of activity, that word is sure to get to those charged with enforcing the imperial decrees. You *cannot* continue as before. Have you not heard what has taken place in Antioch, when the Emperor ordered Juventinus and Maximos, the two soldiers under his command who were followers of the Way, to violate their belief? They refused to defile the food of others with the blood from idol worship, so Emperor Julian, right there in front of everyone in the market, had them put to death! He then ordered their bodies left to rot! Do you want the same end?" There was silence. We were in the courtyard, which had often been a place of joy and peace. It looked the same as before, but the world around it had changed.

Paul stood up and strode over to the fountain. "I am a man!" he exclaimed, opening his arms. "I cannot bend as the wind blows. I will not give up this new hope due to a decree which could change tomorrow! John, what do you think?" he asked, fixing his gaze at me.

I realized then that our lives could completely alter,

depending on what answer I would give. In an instant, I gazed at my own heart and stood. "I too have to be true to the new hope, which has changed everything. If I must pay something back for all I have been given, so be it. But I will not turn my back or cower. I never have, and I will not do so now to any opponent."

Crispinianus had been quiet. He turned to Paul and said, "Do not renounce the new Way! None of us will go backwards on this road; you know that as you know us. But just be careful. Of all here, you are most at risk. We rejoice in Commander Gallicanus who has joined us, but this has put both of you under the attention of the magistrates. Besides this, you are the most popular men in Rome! Even those who don't follow the Way count themselves as your friends!" Everyone chuckled at this and the tension diminished. Throughout this discussion, Benedicta had said nothing. She was like that: strong yet quiet.

"Come, lets us walk," Paul said, as we all left to stroll through that wonderful city that we had made our home so many years before.

We no longer spoke of these things as we passed the buildings, markets, and vendors on the streets. At the moment, there was nothing else to say, except for each one to look into oneself.

We bade one another goodnight after a while, and Paul and I made our way to the top of the hill, from which we could still hear the voices in the Forum, and crowds lingering in the streets.

"John, do you think we would be singled out as those who do not follow Julian's decree?" Even in the darkness, I could see the concern in his eyes. I shook my head for I was sure of the truth of my answer.

"No. We are but specks in the universe of the Empire. There are many who follow the Way and ignore the worship of the old gods. They are left alone. Why should it be different for us?

After all, we aren't Achilles and Nereus[39], are we?" I said with a smile. It was true that Rome was great and we were small; what was there to be concerned about?

\*\*\*

The following days were peaceful and happy, and we continued our lives as before. Exactly three weeks later, a messenger arrived at our door asking for either Paul or me. The man was from the Proconsul, ordering us to appear the next morning at the office of a magistrate. I shut the door and referred the message to Paul, who wondered what the matter could be in reference to.

"Do you think we have been charged with violating the decree?" I wondered this because there was much fear in the city at that time.

"No, I think not," Paul said. "Perhaps we are to be entrusted with a task, such as accompanying a magistrate outside the city." Because we had many powerful friends who held us in great esteem, Paul hoped for the best, but I feared the worst.

\*\*\*

Though we had not been in the legion for many years, we dressed as the soldiers that we had been, in order to show our loyalty to the office of the Emperor. We reported at the magistrate's headquarters which was in a large building near the Forum of Caesar. It was still early morning, with few about yet but the sellers. "Come," we were told by the same messenger who had appeared at our door, a very short man wearing the garb of the legion. We were ushered down a corridor into a room where we stood facing a large chair. We were made to wait for a

---

[39] Achilles and Nereus, martyrs, were members of Rome's Praetorian Guard who were put to death in about 100 C.E. They were buried in the catacombs of Domitilla and their cult was very popular at this time.

long time, until the magistrate entered. As we turned in his direction, our faces turned white.

"Terentianus Verus," I said, surprised. He then smiled a smile which expressed his complacency in having power over us.

"It has come to my attention," he began, "that, notwithstanding the blessed Julian's decree that the ancient gods are to be worshiped, you have persisted in this other Way, and refuse to obey that Emperor, whom you honor with your dress, but not with your lives. I have been given the responsibility to enforce his will in Rome, and what I have heard of you has caused me great disquiet. Your example is looked upon and followed by many. You have even infected Consul Gallicanus, we have heard. For this reason, I am ordering you to return to the gods of old so that Rome might be great once more, to honor our glorious Emperor. Only thus can you save your way of life. And believe me, our blessed Julian will not hesitate to deal with those who refuse his decrees, in the same way that Nero and Diocletian and others have dealt with their enemies." Through this whole monologue we were silent; finding Terentianus Verus here was unexpected. He knew both of us well; he knew we would never go back on any decision. This was and is the men we are. Terentianus seemed to rejoice in the possibility that he could do us further evil.

When he was finished, he dismissed us. As we walked out the door, Paul uttered, under his breath, "We're finished!"

It was obvious that Terentianus took pleasure in his new ability to rule over the lives of men. "Why does he detest us?" I asked Paul, as we made our way through the now busy streets toward our home.

"Because he is only half a man; he is not loved, nor even esteemed, by any. He must crush those who have what he cannot." Paul paused to reflect, then continued, "He desires power above all things, John. He believes he can obtain greater favor in the eyes of the new Emperor if he strictly applies the decrees. And in our case, because he saw us as an obstacle to his power, he will apply the decrees with great force, and with great pleasure." We stopped in a narrow street and faced each other in silence. After a moment Paul's tone changed, as he asked, "John, what should we do?"

I thought for a moment, for I was deeply disturbed also. "Let us seek out the elders tonight, to gain counsel. Perhaps this is not as great a concern as it appears." I hoped my words were true.

\*\*\*

When darkness fell, we sought out Cornelius, Maximus, and Gallus, along with our friend Benedicta. We explained the entire morning encounter to them. Cornelius had now known us for many years, and I directed my question to him. "We need to know what to do!" Cornelius gazed at me a long time, it seemed, and looked over at Paul, who was sitting next to Benedicta. We were in her home, in a small room lit by one lamp. "Paul, John," Cornelius began, "no man can tell you what you should do. But there is only one question you can ask yourself when faced with this or any other difficulty. It is this. "Where lies your hope?" He paused, then added, "That is all there is to be said," and he rose, embraced us firmly, and left.

It had been easy to tell Crispinianus, Benedicta, and Crispus some weeks previously that we would always be loyal to the Way. Then we were pledging our fidelity to an idea. Suddenly the idea had become real, and our decision concerning this could cause us to lose all we had gained. As I slept, I could not get the words of Cornelius out of my mind: "Where lies your hope?"

"John, let us walk," Paul said that next morning. He had slept as little as I, and we both needed to consider everything that was at hand. Without knowing how, we found ourselves in that same place we had been at the beginning of this journey: the tomb of Peter. Many years before, it had been a humble grave, but now the glorious Emperor Constantine had erected a great basilica in its place. The new, white columns gleamed in the morning sun, as some made their way through its bronze doors to that place of peace within. Paul and I did the same, as I remembered our ponderings on that spot that first time, when the idea of loving a god seemed an absurdity. I chuckled to myself now, thinking back on my state of mind then. We made our way to that area in which the apostle was entombed. As I thought of the apostle's fears, I felt the same. I would not turn back, but neither did I want to proceed forward. If the danger grew, I was determined to face it, yet I was equally determined not to be overcome by it. The course of action before us was clear and obscure at the same time. But thinking of the apostle before us, I could sense the same conflict in him. He sought to flee, yet returned to stay. Why? Echoes of our first visit here returned to me as we looked at this spot where he lay. I had almost formulated that word, that driving force that led Peter to this spot, to this sacrifice, when Paul anticipated my thought as he said, "Perhaps it all comes down to this." With these words we returned home, firm in that path that we had begun there so many years before.

***

Fulvia rushed over the next day when she had heard about the threat to us. The garden in which we sat was absent of the joy from her last visit. "John," she pleaded with me, "do as the decree states! You do not have to believe what you do in your heart. You can obey the decree and still believe in the new Way." But Fulvia knew me well, and realized, even as she spoke, that I could not deceive with my actions or with my words. She began to weep. "Please, I'm frightened for you! I don't want any harm to befall you again! Losing you to Egypt was difficult enough. Losing you again would be unbearable!" She continued in this way for a long time, weeping in my arms. To see her so distraught pained me above everything else, but I had no words to console her. I did not know the future or the consequences of my following the new Way. I did know, however, that I could not bend to the decree.

"Fulvia, I love you, and I hate to see you in pain. I know that whatever trials await us, we will be given the strength to overcome them. I want for you to have this hope, too. Do not be distraught, for nothing but a warning has befallen us yet, and perhaps nothing else will." With these words we embraced before she left.

That same evening Crispinianus, Benedicta, and Crispus came to our home. "What can we do to help you?" they asked.

"Your friendship is enough for us," Paul answered.

"We will come to you every day, to pray with you, to sustain you, and to walk this path with you," Benedicta said. She spoke so rarely, that when she did her words were full of meaning. Our bond with them gave us even greater strength, just as the sight of our comrades fighting alongside us in battle had given us courage in the past.

With our faith in the Christus and with the love of our friends, we indeed did walk this path, for we continued our activities as before, as if there were no decree at all. Until one week later.

There was no knock, as ten men of the Roman century burst through our door. Paul and I were ready to mount a fight, being still practiced in battle. But this was not an attack, but an arrest; we allowed ourselves, therefore, to be led to an uncertain fate. As we descended the hill, Paul was taken in one direction and I in another. We were imprisoned in different locations.

These events bring me to the present moment. I write these words as I sit within my cell, filled with many others who were charged with various transgressions of the law. I will not describe the difficulties and uncertainties of my imprisonment. My greatest suffering, however, is the separation from Paul, and not knowing his fate. For several weeks I have been confined, with no one stating the charges, or even communicating with me. What will happen? What was happening to Paul?

\*\*\*

I have waited here for a fortnight since I wrote my account. Today I received a communication through another prisoner; I do not know how it reached me.

*Fear not, brother. Your friends in the Senate and elsewhere are pressuring for your release. There will be an uprising if any harm comes to you. This should be sufficient to see you returned home quickly. Paul also.*

*Fulvia*

I rejoiced in my sister's words, and continued to offer prayers to the Christus in whom I put all my hope.

\*\*\*

I continue to write this account from our home. It is now three days since my release from confinement. What had begun as an account of how I ended up as a criminal continues now that I have been set free. The most recent events unfolded in this way.

I held onto the words of Fulvia, but I also prepared myself for whatever would happen. The Christus had given us so much, and I had given so little in return, that I prepared myself to offer what sacrifice I could in gratitude. Such was my state of mind when a guard approached my cell, opened the door, and said, "You can return home." It seemed that I was in a daze as I was walked into the sunlight for the first time in many days. The first person I saw was Paul; his release had taken place several hours before, and he made his way to where I was being held. There are no words that can capture the emotion of the moment that I saw him, and despite myself, he and I both wept. When I looked beyond him, there were some fifty of our friends, including Fulvia, who greeted us with joy, and wept also. We were very grateful for our release, and the rejoicing was great, with cries and singing. On our arrival, Gallicanus had quickly prepared a feast for all. As the word of our release circulated, by the evening hours there were over a hundred fifty people crowded into our home, wishing us well, and expressing their gratitude and affection. In them, the Christus continued to embrace us. It was late at night when the last of them left. We were exceedingly happy.

It was Fulvia who appeared the next morning to explain how our friends had influenced the Senate to intercede on our behalf. There was fear that any violence done to us would result in bloodshed in the streets, and this is a factor that led to our release without harm. "Come, let us enter our piece of paradise," I said. At this, my sister, Paul, and I sat down in that place of peace, the garden within the center of our home.

Fulvia asked, "Will you not leave Rome for a while, for the sake of safety? I have already spoken with Crispus, and his relatives can host you in Malta for as long as you like. When things calm down, then you can return to the city. What do you think?" I realized that she made this offer from love, and I leaned over and kissed her head, as was my custom. But I knew myself, as well as Paul, and neither of us had ever fled an enemy, real or imagined. We would not do so now. I am sure my sister knew this, for she understood my answer before I said a word.

Before we knew it, Benedicta called on us, and came to the garden, accompanied by Gallicanus. She seemed delighted to stay with us as we sat there enjoying ourselves, with the sunlight pouring in from above. In the meantime, Gallicanus went off to prepare another feast; for him, every day was to be a feast with rejoicing now that we were home.

"Beginning tomorrow," Paul began, "we will continue our

life as before. I wish to help the elders with the *diakonia* and the distribution of bread, and you can tell the elders, Benedicta, that they can meet at our home. Nothing has changed, and because we have friends in the Senate, perhaps we will be secure from further harassment." Benedicta wrinkled her forehead; apparently she did not like what Paul had said, but consented to carry the message. I agreed that our lives must continue as before. We sought to be true to our commitment as we had been our entire lives in the face of any enemy.

# Chapter 12: Fulvia's Account

I am Fulvia, sister of John, sister in spirit of Paul, and have found the manuscript of my brother, resolving to finish his account so that others may know of their lives. What I write here, I have either witnessed myself, or have been told by others who were direct witnesses.

While in the garden on that day that my brother described, I wanted to know the details of their release, which John left out of his account. I knew there was more to their being set free than the door being opened and their being sent home. "What were you told before you were let go?" I asked both of them.

John and Paul glanced at each other, and Paul replied, "We were given a warning." As he said these words, I saw my brother shake his head, in order to make Paul stop. I insisted on knowing what could befall them. John was adamant that no details be given, but the more he refused, the more I needed to know.

Finally, reluctantly, he said, "You may tell her, Paul." So Paul began the account.

"We were told, by order of Terentianus, taking his authority from the Emperor, that if we did not obey the decree, if we persisted in the new Way and rejected the ancient gods, that we would not only lose our freedom, but our lives." My heart fell at these words, for we were again where we were before. A threat was over their heads, yet they were determined to follow this Way. My brother was loyal, both to his belief, as well as to Paul and all those whom he loved. Paul was the same. Whether this was stubbornness, or a soldier's loyalty, or faith in the Christus, I am not sure. They were so much alike, I remember thinking at that moment. At times, it seemed they were the same person in two bodies.

In the days that followed, the two continued as before, with their public involvement in the *diakonia* and hosting the breaking of the bread in their home, as if nothing had happened. If they had fear, they put something else above this. Perhaps this is a soldier's prerogative that I do not understand. In any event, their public following of the Way was not surprising to any who knew them.

It was several days later that their two friends Crispus and Crispinianus arrived, out of breath from rushing across the city with news. "The decrees of the Emperor are losing their force. Many have taken heart from your example, and continue their honor of the Christus as before, ignoring the ancient gods and new laws. It is believed that the laws will be struck down, for they have no force, and most feel they will not dare to arrest others, nor risk an uprising!" They rejoiced at these words, as did I, for it would mean the end to concerns about their safety.

When I arrived home, I asked my husband, who was now in the Senate, about the status of the decree. "What the people want to be true is not always so," he replied. "The enforcement of the decrees will either increase, or they will fade away. These are the two possibilities. It is too soon to see which way the Emperor or magistrates will go." I did not sleep the night my husband spoke these words.

A week passed and all of our lives seemed to return to normal. Benedicta, Crispinianus, and Crispus continued to check daily on their esteemed friends, and I looked in on them whenever I could take leave of my responsibilities. All seemed well, and all of our daily lives continued as before. John and Paul seemed joyful, with no sign of fear on their faces or in their words. This made me feel more at peace, and I began to think that the danger had passed.

Unbeknownst to all, the magistrate in charge of the decrees had been scheming on how to end the influence that John and Paul had on the people. He thought that, by doing so, he would glorify himself. My brother had spoken of the hatred of this man; he was the one responsible for John's exile in Egypt. I recalled that John was perplexed that one could live so long in anger and darkness. In any event, his plan formulated, soldiers blinded by their own obedience were sent to carry out his secret plot.

Exactly ten days after their release from prison, in the middle of the night while the city slept, a group of soldiers burst into the dwelling of John and Paul to seize them and carry out their evil commands. Because the house was large, there were many rooms, with several avenues of escape. Startled awake, the two investigated the noise, and saw the soldiers within their dwelling, but on the lower level. Realizing what was unfolding, they made their way toward another exit, where they could possibly escape before the house was surrounded. As the soldiers ran up the stairs toward that place where they were, John and Paul made for the exit. The soldiers entered the quarters with swords drawn, and were in sight of the two. It became clear that this was to be more than an imprisonment. There was a standoff as everyone froze. This was the moment of their decision, a split second and they could jump to the floor below and escape out a back way. In that instant, Paul grabbed John and said with urgency, "If we submit to this, we will be together forever in paradise." At these words they stopped, turned toward the soldiers, and allowed themselves to be taken.

"You thought you would escape the Emperor's decree," began the Commander, a short, dirty man who spoke as one who feared. "Tonight you will lose everything! Your lives will be dispensed with in secret; your friends cannot stop us now! And word will be given that you fled, renounced all of your beliefs and possessions, begged for mercy, and were granted exile. You will be seen as traitors by all, including your friends who dare go against the decree!" This guard, whose name I do know, but will not record here, continued to try to demoralize the two, who seemed to have no fear, either of his words or of his actions. This infuriated him more. They stood there in certainty, imparting to one another the strength to leap together into the life beyond.

Perhaps he tired of speaking, or perhaps he had expected the two to beg for their lives. In any event, his words fell to the ground. He ordered the executions, but I cannot write the details, for it is a source of too much pain. John and Paul accepted their deaths with courage, certain of the truth of their last words.[40]

\*\*\*

In order for the execution to remain undiscovered, the two were buried within their own home; a deep hole was dug and stones were placed on top. Soldiers were posted to remain in the dwelling in order to keep it secure until the false news of their exile could be spread. But the evil of the Emperor's decree, as carried out by the magistrate Terentianus, did not end here.

The next day, as was their custom, Benedicta, Crispinianus, and Crispus, made their way to the home of John and Paul. On their arrival, they noticed that no one seemed to be present. Both the windows and the door were sealed. Crispinianus grew alarmed and wanted to call for help, but to whom? Gallicanus would not arrive until later in the day; only he could let them inside. But they could not wait to locate him. "We must enter, to find them, or to discover what has transpired," said Benedicta. They were unaware of what danger awaited them. They knew the house well, and made their way to another entrance in back, not knowing that two remaining soldiers were within. They entered the dwelling, the guards remaining unaware of their

---

[40] *Acta SS. Joannis et Pauli*, 4-6. John and Paul were beheaded in their home on the Caelian hill in Rome on June 26, 362 C.E.

entry, to observe what had taken place.

The three friends, not finding John or Paul, eventually made their way to the room where the execution took place. "Behold!" Crispinianus cried out, as they discovered blood on the floor and spattered on the far wall. They found a trail of blood, in fact, and followed it to the area in which the two were entombed. At this moment, the soldiers reacted to Crispinianus' cry and stepped out and surrounded them.

"Now you also must perish!" one cried. In order to preserve the secret of the killing of my brother and Paul, the lives of Benedicta, Crispus, and Crispinianus were also taken on that day. In this way the three, who loved John and Paul so much, joined them in the afterlife, leaving me alone to write these words.[41]

***

I, of course, was unaware of what had transpired the night before, and that next morning I was helping my husband and my youngest son to ready themselves for the day. I had planned to visit John and Paul in the afternoon. In fact, I had prepared a fruit dish which they both enjoyed in the past. Busy with these things, I was startled by a frantic knocking at the door. My heart leapt in fear as I turned and ran to open it. There stood Gallicanus, my brothers' servant, white as snow. I had never seen him manifest any emotion at all, but as he stood there looking at me, and I at him, he suddenly burst into tears, which became a sobbing as he tried to put into words what had taken place. But I needed no words to learn that John and Paul had been slain. I began to weep also and sank down to the ground, unable to rise, unable to speak. My husband and my other children were soon at my side, but I could not see them, my sorrow was so great. I took the hand of Gallicanus and we

---

[41] *Acta SS. Joannis et Pauli,* 6.

looked at each other, sobbing. He began to speak through his pain words that rent my heart even further. "Benedicta, Crispus, and Crispinianus also!"

I believe I screamed, for a crowd gathered round. I yelled, I sobbed. I remember saying, "No, no, no!" over and over. My husband held me, but everyone around seemed only a shadow. My husband begged me to go inside, called on our eldest son to watch over me, and made his way to the home of John and Paul to discover what had taken place.

I insisted on following my husband despite my son's objections, and accompanied by Gallicanus, made my way to that place which had so many memories of joy. Now there was a guard posted, ordering all who ventured to keep away by order of the local magistrate.

Returning home, my husband brought me the news of the attempt at a cover up. He cautioned Gallicanus not to speak publicly about what he had seen inside the house until we were sure that his safety could be assured. I too begged Gallicanus to remain silent, at least for the time being. He remained with me that day, as we mourned those we loved so much.

\*\*\*

Terentianus was still hoping to keep the whole affair quiet when word was brought to him that the three others had also been slain. He became exceedingly annoyed, for his plan had gone awry, and now, with the death of five, it would be impossible to keep the entire affair a secret. Calling his soldiers back, he released the false report that John and Paul had fled, but none believed it. He said nothing of the disappearance of the others. The truth of the death of John and Paul, as well as that of Benedicta, Crispus, and Crispinianus, came to be known by all within days.

There was no uprising, but many came to visit the house of my brothers, to pray to them, to derive courage from their example, and to show disobedience to the unjust decrees. I marveled at how many who loved them in life continued to do so in death.

Because the dwelling was left to my son Pachamius, he made that part of the house in which their lives had been taken a fitting shrine and place of peace for all who would visit. There are many who come, even those whom my brothers never met.

At times I find myself here in the evening, when none are present, and go to that same room and weep for those I love. I sit in that garden which we had enjoyed so much together, and I can almost hear their words, and feel my brother's hand. They live on in the hearts of many who admire their courage and that affection which bound them to one another and to their Christus. I am here, and I long for my brother, and I find myself hoping that what he believed is indeed true.

# Acknowledgments

Both the *Vita Constantini* and the *Passio Joannis et Pauli* are ancient sources, but are more panegyric than historical. Documents of this nature tend to show the concerns of the writer rather than the actual events described. However, some facts can be gleaned from their pages, which I have incorporated here. I have also derived inspiration from the *Acta SS. Nerei et Achillei*, whose lives echo those of John and Paul.

The excavations under the church of St. John and Paul in Rome furnish a wealth of information on John and Paul and are the foundation upon which this story is built.

For Constantine and his time I highly recommend Michael Grant's *Constantine the Great; the Man and His Times* (Charles Scribner's Sons, New York, 1993). He sorts through many of the myths and interpretations of this man, and presents a likely portrait of Constantine. There are other reliable studies on Constantine which I have used here, including *Constantine the Great* by John Holland Smith (Charles Scribner's Sons, New York, 1971) and G.P. Baker's *Constantine the Great and the Christian Revolution* (Cooper Square Press, New York, reprint, 1992).

Though Constantina is painted as a blood thirsty Fury by the Roman historian Ammianus Marcellinus, and as a virgin saint by the medieval author Jacobus de Voragine, I have chosen the middle ground. Most likely she was a pawn within a family that sought to rule the Empire for generations.

For the situation in the first era of Christianity, there is no more valuable source than the series of *Early Church Fathers* by Philip Schaff (Christian Classics Ethereal Library, Grand Rapids, MI, reprint, 1989). The writings are infused with a freshness that is unparalleled.

For Italian sources, I have used Carlo Pavia's *Guida dei Mitrei di Roma Antica* (Gangemi Editore, Rome, 1999) which is a wonderful dialogue between a Christian and a follower of Mithras, comparing the similarities and differences in ancient Rome. *I Culti Orientali a Roma* (in Roma Archeologica, Itenerario 21, Elio de Rosa Editore, Roma, 2004) is a brief but useful guide to the cults of ancient Rome. *Il Titolo di Pammachio Santi Giovanni e Paolo* (by Bianca Maria Margarucci Italiani, Produzione Gen. Dei PP. Passionisti, Rome, 1985) is a useful account of John and Paul. Her bibliography has several interesting sources in Italian.

There are few serious studies in English on the Mithraic cult. *The Mysteries of Mithra* by Franz Cumont (Open Court, Chicago, 1903) is considered a classic, though some of its conclusions are contradicted by newer studies. *The Roman Cult of Mithras* by Manfred Clauss is an excellent modern presentation. Most helpful of all for understanding the cult of Mithras are the excavations in Rome under St. Clements, Santa Prisca, and the many found in Ostia.

For the Roman legions I found Adrian Goldsworthy's *The Complete Roman Army* (Thames and Hudson, London, 2003) full of interesting information, as well as Adrian Goldsworthy's *Roman Warfare* (Harper Collins, Great Britian, 1999). The short but informative *Le legioni di Roma* by Anna Maria Liberati e Francesco Silverio (Fratelli Palombi Editori, Rome, 1990) gives a good overview of a soldier's daily life as well as methods of battle.

For her knowledge and expertise, I thank Roman archeologist Marina Giustini. For his loyalty and expertise, I express my gratitude to my editor Paul F. Keaveney.

Printed in Great Britain
by Amazon

33480928R10106